SARANORMAL

HAUNTED MEMORIES

by Phoebe Rivers

SIMON SPOTLIGHT
New York London Toronto Sydney New Delhi

SIMON SPOTLIGHT
An imprint of Simon & Schuster Children's Publishing Division
1230 Avenue of the Americas, New York, New York 10020
Copyright © 2012 by Simon & Schuster, Inc.
All rights reserved, including the right of reproduction in whole or in part in any form.
SIMON SPOTLIGHT and colophon are registered trademarks of Simon & Schuster, Inc.
Text by Heather Alexander
For information about special discounts for bulk purchases, please contact Simon & Schuster
Special Sales at 1-866-506-1949 or business@simonandschuster.com.
Manufactured in the United States of America 0312 OFF
First Edition 10 9 8 7 6 5 4 3 2 1
ISBN 978-1-4424-5381-4 (hc)
ISBN 978-1-4424-4040-1 (pbk)
ISBN 978-1-4424-4041-8 (eBook)
Library of Congress Catalog Card Number 2012931141

CHAPTER 1

No one saw me.

I pressed my back against the pale-green cafeteria wall. How long would it be before anyone noticed I existed? Minutes? Hours? Days? The entire school year?

Yesterday was different. Everyone smiled. New clothes. New haircuts. New binders. Blank paper organized perfectly into labeled sections. Even teachers smiled, swept up in the great-to-be-back vibe.

There were a lot fewer smiles today. The second day.

By now Stellamar Middle School was old news to everyone—except me. I gnawed my bottom lip, pretended to smooth wrinkles on my favorite sky-blue top, and scanned the cafeteria.

I don't belong here. I'm not one of them, I thought. My

stomach twisted nervously. *Can they see I'm different? Can they sense it?*

I choked back a laugh. *Seriously, Sara. Stop being silly,* I scolded myself. *No one senses anything. They don't even notice you.*

Yesterday I spent lunch in the guidance office as they sorted out my records from my old school. I wondered if I should head back there. Create another problem for them to solve.

Hide.

"Oh, wow! Can you believe Mrs. Moyers kept me after class? I mean, it's the second day. Like I really need a reminder not to speak without raising my hand. Come on, we're in seventh grade." Lily Randazzo rushed through the cafeteria door, her long black hair flying behind her. She scooped her arm through mine and propelled me into the lunchroom.

I hurried to keep up as she expertly wove her way around kids wandering aimlessly with plastic lunch trays.

"You don't have her, do you?" Lily continued, not stopping to say hi or even breathe. "I wish we had more classes together. Oh, hey, Erin!" She waved at a short girl with a high ponytail. "But you like it here, right? All's good, right?"

"Sure." I wasn't sure, but I didn't know what else to say. At the moment, I was just grateful to be wrapped in the whirlwind of Lily.

"There's barely any time to eat," Lily announced to a long table filled with girls. "Scoot down, Avery, okay?"

"Sure thing." Avery smiled, showing off a rainbow of rubber bands on her braces.

"Can you push down for Sara, too?" Lily asked. "She just moved to my street this summer. Everyone, this is Sara." Lily pointed to me.

My face grew warm as the girls stopped eating and stared. I wasn't like Lily, who loved attention. I was happier on the edge of a crowd. But I liked Lily, and I wanted her friends to like me. "Hi," I managed. My voice sounded unnaturally squeaky.

I quickly slid onto the bench next to Lily. Avery leaned across Lily's sandwich and squinted at me with slate-gray eyes. "You're really pretty," she said finally. From the way she said it, I wasn't sure if it was a compliment or an accusation.

"Oh . . . thanks." I pulled out my container of

mixed-berry yogurt and tried to be friendly. "I like your braces."

"I decided to go all Roy G. Biv. You know, the total rainbow." Avery flashed a full-tooth grin. She had a different color rubber band on each tooth. The effect was a bit dizzying.

"Sara looks like that because she's from California," Miranda announced. She sat across from Avery. I'd met Miranda a few weeks ago on the boardwalk with Lily, but I didn't know her well.

"That makes no sense, Miranda," scoffed a thin girl with wavy, reddish hair. "Not everyone from California has long blond hair and blue eyes like Sara. There's no way everyone in California is, like, that pretty."

All the girls stared at me again. I didn't know what to say. I didn't want to talk about how I looked. I studied my pink yogurt.

"That's true. There are ugly people in California too," Lily piped in. "But Sara looks like a surfer girl. I mean, wouldn't you cast her in one of those sunscreen commercials? She'd be great in that new one with that girl on the paddleboard."

Everyone agreed with Lily. I swirled the yogurt

with my plastic spoon as they discussed the best commercials.

"Why did you move to New Jersey?" Avery asked.

"My father got a new job," I explained, relieved at the change in subject. I told them a little about his job and our move. I didn't tell them that he'd been fired from his old job or that his girlfriend had dumped him. I didn't tell them that I still couldn't figure out why we had to suddenly move across the country when life seemed perfectly okay in California.

But I was used to keeping information to myself.

Miranda and Lily gave me a rundown on all the teachers. Who was supposed to be tough and who favored the girls over the boys. The other girls jumped in with stories and warnings. The way they talked over one another, filling in sentences and laughing, made it clear they'd been friends for a long time. Everyone seemed to have some zany story or advice they wanted to share. I began to relax.

"Look who's checking out Sara," the red-haired girl, whose name was Tamara, suddenly whispered. She gave a slight nod to her right. Immediately every girl at our table whipped her head to the right.

"Oh, that was subtle!" Tamara cried.

Everyone giggled. I gazed in that direction. A table of boys.

"Who?" Miranda demanded. "Who was looking?"

"All of them," Tamara said. "They all want to see who the new girl is." She leaned across the table toward me. "I think Luke's especially interested."

"Who?"

"The boy with the dark-blond hair," Lily whispered.

There were at least four boys with dark-blond hair. None of them were looking at me.

I shrugged. I didn't care about boys. I was just happy Lily had saved me from being the weird kid in the corner.

"Your friends are nice," I said to Lily.

"You fit right in," she whispered to me. "I knew you would."

I smiled as I tossed my empty yogurt container back in my brown paper bag and pulled out a yellow pear. I listened as Lily showed Miranda the thin bangle bracelets she had layered on her wrists. My thumb pressed the pear's too-soft flesh, adding another bruise to its dented skin. The pear's musky, overripe scent filled my nose and I pushed it, uneaten, back into the bag. Gross! I hated mushy fruit. Crumpling the bag, I stood to toss it into the trash can.

"Stop right there," a harsh voice demanded after I'd taken only a few steps. "Are you *really* going to do that?"

I turned and saw the scowling face of an overweight man. Unruly gray eyebrows framed his narrowed eyes. He wore a shiny navy polyester tracksuit with white stripes down the arms and legs. The jacket was partially unzipped, and his belly strained against a worn gray T-shirt. "Me?" I asked, looking around. Was he talking to *me*?

"You heard me," he continued, his tone gruff. He pointed to my arm, the one that held the lunch bag. "It's wrong. A crime."

I swallowed hard. I didn't know what he was talking about. "W-what did I do?"

"In this school, we don't stand for that kind of behavior," the man continued. "Not in my room. Do you know you are in my room? I may be a gym teacher, but I am also in charge of the cafeteria. My room, my rules."

My head bobbed up and down, as if no longer

attached to my neck. Agreeing with him. About what I didn't know. I just wanted to go back to my table.

"Your actions deserve a detention." He reached into his jacket pocket, pulling out a yellow pad and the kind of short green pencil you get at mini-golf.

I swallowed hard. *Detention? Me?* I'd never gotten into trouble in my old school. I glanced toward Lily. She was busy talking to Avery and hadn't noticed this teacher yelling at me.

He began to write on the pad. "Name?" he demanded.

I gnawed my lip. I couldn't get in trouble. Not me. "What did I do?" I asked again. My voice wavered as my heart pounded.

"I asked for your name." The gym teacher glared at me.

"Sara Collins." I stared down at my red Converse sneakers, feeling my cheeks burning. What would I tell my dad? I couldn't make sense of what was happening. "But why—?" I gazed back up at the gym teacher. The air around me grew thick. Heavy.

"You're new, Sara Collins," he growled. He scratched his balding head with the tip of the stubby pencil.

"Yes—" I couldn't bring him into focus. He shimmered before me, an undulating blob of blue.

"Sara, why are you hanging by the garbage can?" A voice floated toward me. Avery. Or maybe Tamara. I couldn't be sure. My pulse quickened as spots of light danced before me.

"Do you know why you are getting a detention, Sara Collins?" the gym teacher asked.

I gasped for air. I tried to slow my breathing. Something was wrong.

"You are getting a detention because you have given in to pear pressure."

My throat tightened. Dry. My mouth was so dry. I tried to bring him into focus. Tried to stop the pulsing light.

"Peer pressure. *Pear* pressure! You see? It's a pun!" And with that, he doubled over in deep laughter. "Gotcha!"

I tried to stop the familiar swaying I felt inside. The tingling running up my leg. Reaching back, my hand grasped the plastic garbage can. I held on tight.

"Gotcha!" he bellowed again. "I saw you with that pear!"

I widened my eyes and stared. His body was now completely transparent. I could see *through* him.

I squeezed my eyes tight. *Please, not here. Not now.*

I prayed it wasn't true. But I knew it was.

The gym teacher wasn't alive. He wasn't here.

Not really.

"What's Sara doing?" I heard the voice in the distance. One of the girls.

"You don't think I'm funny? Come on . . . that was a classic fruit joke. Admit it," the gym teacher said, his body still shimmering before me. Here and not here. "You're not mad about the detention thing, are you?" The gym teacher now looked concerned. Transparent and concerned.

"Yes, I'm mad," I whispered. "Why are you doing this to me?"

He shrugged. "You can see me."

I swallowed hard. I hadn't been expecting an answer.

"Leave me alone!" I hissed through gritted teeth.

"Why is Sara talking to that garbage can? She's not talking to a garbage can, is she, Lily?" I could hear their voices. They saw. Well, not all of it. I knew they couldn't see the dead guy. Only *I* saw the dead people.

But they saw enough to make sure I'd never fit in here. Weird girl.

"I sensed it immediately," he said.

I knew I shouldn't speak. I knew I should walk away. Go back to the girls and make a joke about talking to myself. I knew it. I really did. Yet somehow I couldn't leave.

"Sensed what?" I asked. His body continued to flicker in and out of focus, yet the suffocating feeling was fading.

"You have the gift."

I rubbed the hangnail on my thumb, not sure what to say. I wasn't surprised. Not really. I've seen spirits since I was little. I've never told anyone, not even my dad. Then last month, when I moved to this shore town, something strange happened. I started *really* seeing spirits. Everywhere. And hearing them. I'd never heard them speak before.

Now this guy. Playing jokes on me and having a conversation.

"We have a connection. You and I," the gym teacher said gleefully, pointing to me.

I couldn't let this happen here. New school. A

chance to be normal. I shook my head defiantly. "No, no, we don't!" I cried.

I loosened my grip on the trash can and willed my feet to move back to the table.

"Sara, were you just yelling at the trash can?" Avery couldn't control her giggles.

All the girls eyed me oddly. Even Lily. I glanced back at the trash can. The gym teacher's spirit was still there. Hovering.

I took a deep breath. "Just practicing for a . . . summer vacation speech I have to give in class later." Lying was not my thing. "Do you guys have it too?"

No one, of course, knew about a speech.

"Oh, maybe it was just for me because I'm new. . . ." I gratefully allowed myself to be swallowed into their group, as we headed out of the cafeteria into the halls.

I needed to be much more careful, I realized. I was on the verge of having a group of friends, and I desperately wanted to hang on to them.

I had to keep the dead people far away from the living.

That meant no more talking to spirits in school.

CHAPTER 2

"There's nothing to do here. It's old and kind of empty," I apologized. "It's not fun like your house."

I glanced nervously across our wide porch as I crossed to the front door. The spirit of the old woman sat on the double swing, where she'd always been ever since I moved in. Knitting needles clacking. Fingers moving furiously. I knew Lily couldn't see her, but still I wished she wasn't there.

"You think my house is fun? It's crazy. My brothers and Cammie never leave us alone," Lily complained. "Besides, I've been waiting so long for you to ask me over." She grinned. "Was it bad that I invited myself? My mom would freak. No manners."

I shook my head. "No, it's fine." I loved the chaos of Lily's house. With five kids and an endless supply of cousins, there was always noise and excitement. Nothing like my family. Only child. One parent. Very quiet.

"Do you—" I hesitated. Lily had stepped toward the large bay window alongside the door to better examine the dark purple letters outlined in brilliant gold on the wooden sign: LADY AZURA: PSYCHIC, HEALER, MYSTIC.

"It's so cool," she breathed. "I'm kind of scared but kind of excited to see her. She's home, right?"

"Yeah, she's here. She's always here." I turned my key in the lock and paused before opening the door. "I have to help her after school. Go to the store, around the house, that kind of thing."

"Does she pay you?"

"No." I'd kept a lot about my life secret from Lily. I had no idea how she would feel about Lady Azura. I still had no idea how *I* felt about Lady Azura. "It's part of an arrangement my dad made. We rent the top two floors from her, and my dad helps fix it up, and I . . . well, I go to the store on my bike and, I guess, I just listen to her a lot."

"Sounds great," Lily nodded. "I'll help today too."

I let out a fraction of the breath I was forever

holding in. I shouldn't have doubted Lily. So far, she'd been fine with everything. No matter how strange.

"Oh!" Lily gasped, as the door swung open onto a small, frail woman wearing a long royal-blue caftan embroidered with orange.

"Welcome." Lady Azura reached out and grasped Lily's hand. "I sensed multiple energies approaching. Ah, who are you, my dear? Such dark yet vibrant eyes."

"I'm Lily. Sara's friend."

"Of course you are. And a good friend too. I can sense it." She tottered forward on gold mules with narrow heels, pulling Lily into the large Victorian house.

I watched Lily eye Lady Azura's outfit. Both had a passion for fashion. Lady Azura dressed each day how I imagined someone would who entertained foreign royalty on a yacht in the Mediterranean. Flowing dresses, thick makeup, and crimson lipstick artfully applied. Except for me and a random client or two, I doubted she saw anyone all day. I sometimes wished I could bring her somewhere nice, but I couldn't figure out where that would be in this small town. The pizza place on the boardwalk?

Besides, we didn't have that kind of relationship.

At all.

Lady Azura's eyes sparkled beneath the jet-black fringe of her false eyelashes. "Let's have a snacks party, shall we?" Lily eagerly followed her through the narrow foyer and into the back kitchen. I trailed along.

"Now tell me, what is happening in that school of yours?" Lady Azura placed a pitcher of pink lemonade, a package of Vienna Fingers, and a bowl of Skittles on the table in front of us. She liked sugar.

"Well, it just started last week, so no tests yet." Lily took a sip from her glass and grimaced slightly. Lady Azura always poured too much pink powder into the water. "The Harvest Festival is at the end of the month."

"Of course! Why should anything change?" Lady Azura gave a low chuckle. "Did you know that I was Harvest Queen when I was your age?" A wistful look came over her. "Everyone said my rule was like no other."

Lily leaned across the linoleum table. "I can see you in the tiara and riding on the float."

"Would you like to?" Without waiting for an answer, Lady Azura left the room, heels clicking on the worn wooden floors.

"Harvest what?" I asked. I carefully picked through the bowl, making sure I didn't grab any orange Skittles. Orange candies make me gag.

"Harvest Festival," Lily explained. "Happens every year in Stellamar since, well, I guess since she was young, which is, like, a hundred years ago. There's a huge parade, and one girl is chosen to ride a big float and be queen of the middle school dance. There's lots of other stuff that day too. Carnival games, pie contests, things like that. Most of it is pretty lame."

"Here I am." Lady Azura returned, still steady on heels even though by my dad's guess, she was past eighty. "Walk down memory lane with me for a moment, girls," she said with a smile as she handed us a black-and-white photograph, yellowed with age. A young girl wearing a rhinestone tiara stood on the back of a pickup truck decorated with crepe paper and waved a thin arm as if she were truly royalty. I recognized the girl's determined gaze. Lady Azura hadn't outgrown that.

We listened politely to the story of her victory. "I was special, even back then. I didn't need a crown to prove it, although I do love sparkly accessories.

You realize, of course, I knew I had won before they announced the vote."

"You can see the future? For real?" Lily asked.

"I can see where people are going and the journeys that have led them there," she said.

I tapped the table impatiently. Lady Azura always spoke like this—in riddles. Was she for real or were her powers, as she called them, completely fake? I had no idea.

"Could you tell our futures?" Lily smiled the smile that made teachers want to give her *A*'s and old ladies tell her fortune.

"Certainly, my child." Lady Azura blotted her lips on the paper napkin, leaving behind a thin, uneven red print. "I've already glimpsed Sara's future, though."

"You never told me about that!" Lily turned to me, incredulous.

I wrinkled my nose. "It was nothing. I kind of forgot about it." My eyes wandered down to my sneakers, avoiding her gaze. I hadn't forgotten. In fact, I thought about it all the time. About *him* all the time. "She said I would meet a tall, dark, and handsome boy." It sounded ridiculous when I heard myself say it.

But the vision I'd had of him when Lady Azura pressed a ruby crystal against my palm flashed before my eyes.

More than a vision.

The warmth of his breath as he stood by my locker at school. The faint smell of almond soap mingled with peanut butter. He helped me gather the binders that had tumbled into the hall, his eyes locking with mine. A bond.

I bit my lip. It *wasn't* real, I reminded myself. School had started, and there was no boy who looked like him. No boy who looked at me the way he did. *Lady Azura made it up and you fell for it,* I scolded myself.

I hated that I fell for it. I hated that I tucked the ruby crystal under my pillow and that I slept with it every night. I knew, even tonight, I'd still keep it there. Lady Azura had told me that the ruby crystal would make love bloom. I knew it was nonsense, but a tiny part of me so very much wanted it to be true.

Well, maybe not that tiny a part.

"Follow me." Lady Azura led the way out of the kitchen. "Goodness knows I could use a little practice. It's been weeks now. Summer tourists leave and business dries up." She shook her head. "Seasons come and go and yet we must press on. We must find ways to use our gifts. To remain at our potential."

We pushed through the thick, purple, crushed-velvet curtain that marked the entrance to Lady Azura's rooms. "You never told me—" Lily stared at the room, momentarily speechless. An ornate tapestry patterned with celestial images. A huge crystal ball on a pedestal. Tarot cards arranged in the dim light of a fringed lamp. Twinkling gemstones and mysterious deep-hued liquids in glass bottles. Leather books with golden spines. "Why didn't you tell me? It's amazing."

She was right. With the heavy red curtains drawn over the front windows and the spicy scent of cinnamon from the huge multi-wicked candles, it felt as if we were entering a secret lair filled with promises and possibilities.

"I didn't know if you'd like it too," I admitted.

But there was more to it. Bringing Lady Azura and Lily together was like mixing Mentos with Pepsi. Lily was school and friends and being a normal twelve-year-old. Lady Azura was a kooky woman who promised the supernatural. I didn't really believe she could deliver, but being around her made me acutely aware of *my* secret.

I *could* deliver the supernatural.

Mixing us all together, I feared, could blow up in my face.

The three of us sat at the round table in the center of the room. Lady Azura, perched on the edge of a large armchair, reached across the red tablecloth for Lily's hand. She gently turned it to reveal the network of lines etched into her palm.

The repetitive *tap, tap, tap* of my foot filled the room as Lady Azura bent over, deep in concentration, sorting through the road map of Lily's life.

Bad idea. This is a bad idea. My foot tapped faster.

"Here is your life line." She pointed to a curved line. "You will have many great adventures."

"Really?" Lily peered at her palm as if it were one of those hidden picture puzzles. "What kind?"

Lady Azura's finger traced the faint lines. "You will travel. Many will know you. Your face will be seen far and wide."

Lily sucked in her breath. "I'm going to be famous!"

"Fame is the echo of actions," Lady Azura said in her raspy voice. "There will be a crossroads within the next six months. A time of decision. Choose wisely, my child. Be famous for the right thing." She released Lily's hand.

That was it?

Both feet solidly on the floor now. No more tapping. I'd been worried for nothing.

Stars shone in Lily's eyes. "Did you hear, Sara? I'm going to be *famous*!"

"I know." I didn't have to read Lily's palm to guess she'd be famous. She loved to sing and dance, and she brightened any room she entered. No magic there.

"Let's go up to my room," I offered. "I took some great photos on the beach last week—"

"What's that?" Lily motioned to a cut-crystal bell with a graceful handle that rested on the side of the table.

"This bell"—Lady Azura cupped it protectively—"is for summoning the departed."

"You mean, the dead?"

My brain jumped ahead. We couldn't go there. We just couldn't. I quickly pushed back from the table, nearly knocking my spindly wooden chair to the ground. "Let's go, Lil."

"Yes, the dead," Lady Azura answered. "The bell is a conduit to the past."

Lily remained in her seat, transfixed on the bell. "Can you—? I mean, is it too much to ask to summon a dead . . . a departed person? My grandma Deb." Lily was twitching with excitement. "I've got something to ask her."

"I don't think—," I began, already on my feet.

"Of course, my child. You have such vitality. Together we shall work to reach across the great divide." Lady Azura reached for Lily's hand again. "Sara, why don't you sit?"

"But—"

"Come on, Sara," Lily pleaded, her eyes fixed on Lady Azura and the bell.

I slipped back into my chair. The Skittles were suddenly swirling unpleasantly in my stomach.

Lady Azura stood and switched off the lights, bathing the room in the flickering glow of candlelight. Shadows crept along the walls as she returned to the large chair, shut her eyes, and instructed us to do the same.

Minutes passed in silence. My leg jerked, desperate to resume its soothing *tap, tap, tap*. I concentrated on remaining still. The faster we did this, the faster we could get out of here, I reasoned.

Then I heard the bell. A full-bodied chime. Four times. "We ring this bell to the four corners of the earth. To the four seasons of the year. To the four directions of the wind." She paused. "We wish to contact Deb, beloved grandmother of Lily."

I peeked. Lady Azura's eyes were open, but she stared blankly into the distance, her face empty.

"Deb . . . Deb . . ." Her voice wavered.

My left foot began to tingle. Tiny pinpricks.

"I can sense her presence."

So could I. The nerves along my leg quivered. Mini rubber bands flicking under my skin. The air grew stale. Hot.

"What is your question for Grandma Deb?" Lady Azura remained stiff and detached.

Lily opened her eyes. She frantically searched the dim room. "Is she here?"

"She is." Lady Azura nodded toward the right corner by the shelves.

We both turned. I gulped.

A woman shimmered in the corner, her outline

faint. Fainter than other spirits I'd seen.

Lady Azura has powers! I realized. I couldn't pretend anymore that maybe she didn't. She made a dead person appear!

Lily raised her eyebrows at me, clearly not believing her grandmother was in the room. "Grandma Deb, uh, you know that prize-winning chocolate cake you were so famous for baking?"

I stared at the faded form of Grandma Deb. She had thick hair and wide-set eyes like Lily.

"You never told anyone the secret ingredient, and now no one can make the cake. It would be really nice to bake it to remember you. . . ." Lily's voice trailed off uncertainly.

"The secret ingredient," Lady Azura repeated.

The spirit began to chuckle. "That cake? All these years and you people still care about Deb's cake?"

"Some secrets are dear," Lady Azura was saying to Lily. "Your grandma fears revealing her secret."

"Why?" Lily asked.

I didn't hear the answer. I was listening to the spirit.

"My banana bread was far superior to Deb's cake. But no, people would say, 'Fran, your sister makes the best cake. What's in it?'" The spirit waved her arms, as if gathering oxygen. I pushed my fingernails into my palms as it became hard to breathe.

Lady Azura began to hum. "A spice, she is saying."

The spirit wasn't Grandma Deb, I realized. My lungs contracted painfully.

"Deb thought she was keeping such a big secret . . . sisters know . . ." the spirit ranted.

"I'm losing Grandma Deb," Lady Azura intoned.

Wheezing. I could hear the choked wheezing coming from my mouth. I needed air.

The spirit shook her head. "Tomatoes. Canned tomatoes."

"She says it is an exotic spice—"

"No! It's tomatoes!" I burst out. "It isn't even your grandma. It's her sister, Fran, and she says it was canned tomatoes."

And with that the spirit was gone. Sweet, fresh air filled the room. Filled my lungs.

Lily burst into laughter. "Tomatoes? Sara, you are too funny!"

I licked my dry lips and tried to slow my breathing, to stop wheezing, so I could think clearer.

"It was just a joke," I mumbled.

"How did you know I had a great-aunt Fran?"

I could feel Lady Azura's eyes burning into me. I refused to look at her.

"Your mother . . . um . . . mentioned her once," I fumbled.

Lily shrugged. "Well, that was truly funny." She turned to Lady Azura. "Thanks a lot for trying. I'm sure it's hard to . . . ." Lily stood, unsure how to finish.

I glanced up. A peculiar grin spread across Lady Azura's face. "Sara, may I have a minute? In private?"

"Lily and I have to go to her house," I announced with sudden urgency. "I, uh, left my flip-flops there, and I need them." I grabbed Lily's hand and pushed her through the door.

"Sara." Lady Azura's voice floated after me.

I turned slightly. Lily was already in the foyer.

"I know what you can do."

I didn't answer.

For years I'd wished for someone to share my secret with, someone who would understand. Now Lady Azura knew.

And I was petrified of what came next.

CHAPTER 3

"Do you remember where your locker is? And your first class?" Lily asked as we climbed the concrete steps to the middle school the next morning.

"Got it." I shifted the weight of my canvas book bag. "First period is science. Miss Klingert. Room—" I thought for a minute. "Room 142."

"Okay. I'm impressed." Lily grinned at me. "Much less dazed and confused today."

"What do you mean?" I demanded, searching my wrists for a hair band. Nothing. The six-block walk to school in the early September heat had matted my hair to the back of my neck.

"I'm just saying you seemed a little weird yesterday, that's all." Lily's thick dark hair was tied back in two loose braids. "I never found your flip-flops. I did look."

"That's fine." I felt bad that she'd spent time searching for something I knew was tucked in my closet.

"Oh, hey, look at Tamara's top! I almost bought the same one." She pointed toward a gray-and-purple-striped back already slipping through the front doors. "My cousin Kim works in the store that has it. Maybe I should text her and see if it's still there." Lily grabbed my hand. "Let's see how it looks on Tamara."

We chased her down to where the main hall split into three smaller hallways. I left to find my locker. It looked like all the others. Dull metallic cranberry. Circular combination lock. Number 303.

But when I opened the door, it definitely wasn't like all the others.

I peered inside. Nothing. I hadn't even decorated yet. No photos or mirrors or write-on boards. Just empty metallic walls. And a strange, cold breeze.

Blowing from *inside* my locker.

Other kids squatted alongside their lockers, pushing backpacks in and pulling binders out. No one seemed to be feeling what I felt. Strange.

First-period bell sounded. I slammed the door

shut and, shivering, hurried to science.

Morning announcements were being broadcast on the huge white screen attached to the front wall. I perched on a stool by a lab table, doodling on my notebook.

Community service club. Literary magazine. Parade float-building committee. Should I join something? I wondered. My pen traced the petals of a daisy. Perfect blue-inked ovals and a curlicue stem. I couldn't, I realized. I'd promised to always come home and help Lady Azura.

Lady Azura. The pebbles in my stomach grew into rocks. Heavy with dread. How long could I avoid her? I wondered.

"Today we will be doing our first lab," Miss Klingert announced. She stared expectantly at us. We all stared back, unsure what she was waiting for.

"Our first lab, class." She waved a yellow folder in the air. "Some excitement would be nice."

A bunch of kids cheered. Miss Klingert smiled, encouraged. Her brown hair was clipped back, and she retained the faint glow of a summer tan. "Earth science has great hands-on labs. I assume all of you read the chapter about moon phases in your textbook last night?"

We all waited, perched on stools around lab tables.

"I can't hear you," Miss Klingert chirped, hands on her hips. "Did you read the chapter, class?"

"Yes!" we all chanted.

Miss Klingert beamed. "Excellent!"

"She was definitely a cheerleader when she was in school," a girl behind me whispered to someone.

"Lab partners are listed on this sheet." Miss Klingert waved a piece of paper above her head. "Go to the lab table assigned. I will pass out the materials and the worksheet that must be filled out by both of you. You will both share the grade and need to work closely together. Ready?"

A few kids answered with a halfhearted "Ready."

"I know you can do better than that," Miss Klingert scolded. "Ready?"

"Ready," we all cried.

I made my way to the list slowly. Except for a girl named Marlee who sat at Lily's lunch table, I didn't know anyone.

Sara Collins/Jayden Mendes—Table 3

I turned toward the table by the window, my eyes searching out my lab partner. Two girls on one side and a boy on the other.

A boy.

The boy.

The boy from my vision. Here. Now. Real.

I couldn't move. Just stare. I could only stare at him.

Brown. He looked as if he'd been dipped in brown. Thick brown hair shaggy around the ears. Caramel skin with high cheekbones. Eyes the color of warm brownies. Even a shirt in the same deep hue.

"I think we're partners," the Boy in Brown said.

Jayden. Jayden Mendes was his name according to the lab partners sheet.

I blinked rapidly, trying to kick my brain into action. What did it mean that he was real? He wasn't by my locker like in my vision, but he looked the same. So *was* he the same? Had the ruby crystal under my pillow worked?

"I'm going to just start this lab if you don't . . ."

"No, no. I'm here. I'm good. Ready for moon phases." Suddenly springing into action, I bounded over to the table as I babbled on. "So what's the lab about?"

"The phases of the moon."

Oh, wow. He must really think I'm an idiot. And science is usually one of my best subjects. "I know that. I meant, what's with the Oreos?" I pointed to Miss Klingert depositing handfuls of Oreos along with worksheets to each pair.

"A party?" Jayden counted out the cookies before us, as Miss Klingert explained that we needed to open the Oreo and, using a plastic knife, carve the eight phases of the moon—from new moon to waning crescent—into the cream and then record the data and answer the questions on the sheet.

Jayden eyed me with mock seriousness. "Which of us should carve?" He held out the white plastic knife. "I personally have witnessed many disastrous Thanksgiving turkey carvings by my grandfather. He shreds the bird. We eat it with a spoon. But"—he spoke in an exaggerated deep voice—"I have learned from my ancestor's mistakes."

He was funny. I liked him. "Well, I'm an excellent cupcake froster," I boasted, playing along. "With a plastic knife, I can ice any cupcake anywhere."

"Impressive. Have you been on any cupcake TV shows?"

"No," I admitted. "But I did just move here."

"Aha! I could tell you were new."

"How?"

He sniffed, his nose scrunching in the most adorable way. "You don't smell like salt-water taffy. It's a special odor for locals. All that time spent on the boardwalk."

I pretended to sniff. "I'm not getting taffy from you."

"Because I'm not local either. Moved here last year from Atlanta."

"I see." I reached for an Oreo, twisted off the top cookie, and handed it to him. "I'll open the cookies. You can carve."

"Wise choice, since you have never been on a cupcake show." He opened the textbook, peered at the moon diagrams, and began on the first one. "Double Stuff would have been easier to work with."

"My dad likes to say that sometimes less is more," I teased. I couldn't believe how easily the words were coming to me. I'd never flirted like this with a boy before. Ever.

Jayden's hair flopped in his eyes, and he pushed it away. "Sometimes less is just less. Like with Oreo cream." He held up the first cookie moon. "Does this look like a waxing crescent?"

We worked together on the lab, joking and teasing each other. I forgot he was The Boy. Together we drew diagrams of our cream-moon carvings onto our worksheets. I bent over my paper. I lowered my head. Closer. Squinting to see. The lines and writing were growing fainter.

Had the lights in the classroom dimmed? Had Miss Klingert drawn the shades? I could barely make out the outline of the circles. My pencil scribbled haphazardly as I leaned in even closer.

"Wow, you stink at coloring, Sara. Didn't anyone teach you to stay inside the lines?"

"Don't you think it's dark in here?" I asked.

"Not really." Jayden sped through the worksheet. I stopped writing, wondering whether I had an eye disease. Should I go to the nurse? Shadows lay heavily around me.

"We are awesome," Jayden declared. He jutted his chin toward the girls across from us. "We're almost done, and they haven't even started their questions." He raised his right hand. "Low five, partner."

I raised my hand, and my fingertips grazed his skin. Instantly my body jerked backward. I snatched my hand away, as if jolted by electricity. I twisted about, confused.

My eyes met Jayden's for a second before he looked away. He was confused too. He examined his palm.

I started to speak, but the sudden smell of sour milk made me push my stool back. The stench came from . . . I gazed about. It seemed to come from Jayden. How could that be? I gently covered my nose with my hand, hoping I wasn't being obvious.

A shadow. A darkness.

Someone stood behind Jayden.

The spirit of a teenage boy. He was dressed in a dark hoodie, so it was hard to really see his face, but I could feel his scowl.

He was angry. Angry at me.

He didn't speak. Just scowled. His dislike blanketed me, like the darkness.

The lab ended. We handed in our sheet. No more joking. Jayden hurried off to his next class, and the spirit trailed after him.

Who was that? I wondered, as the odor lifted and the room brightened.

CHAPTER 4

I twirled the stem between my fingers, watching the pale pink ruffles spin. The flower felt as if it had just been pulled from a florist's cold glass case.

I searched again for a note but couldn't find one. *Strange,* I thought, replacing the carnation on the metal shelf and swinging my locker door shut.

It must be Lily, I decided, heading to the cafeteria. Why didn't I think to put something in her locker? Did all the girls here do that? I panicked. I didn't want to be a bad friend.

No one at our lunch table had a flower. Lily sat at the other end, but I didn't call out to her. What if she gave one only to me? I'd thank her later.

"Who do you think is going to be Harvest Queen?" Miranda was asking, as Avery made room for me again.

Posters for the dance had appeared overnight on the walls of the cafeteria.

"Dina Martino, for sure," Tamara said. Other girls nodded.

"She's the most popular eighth grader, but Caroline Melillo is so pretty," Miranda put in.

"It's not about pretty," Lily said from her end. "It's all about the fear factor. Dina is popular, and people are scared that if they don't vote for her, she'll ruin them. Harvest Queen is a stupid popularity contest. She'll win."

"Harvest Queen is more than that," Avery argued. "It's about someone who gives back to the community and represents the virtues of the school."

"Seriously, Aves, did you memorize the posters? No one really believes that. The girls who want to be queen are the self-loving airheads. It's totally an image thing," Miranda said, siding with Lily.

I turned my attention toward the table against the left wall. Dancing queens, or whatever they were, didn't interest me. I didn't know any of the eighth graders. I barely knew the kids in my own classes.

Jayden, the Boy in Brown, was there, except he

wore a navy shirt today. I couldn't stop looking at him. He was so cute. I watched him step toward the table, a tray of food balanced on one hand. The table was packed with boys eating.

"One of us could run," Avery was suggesting. "You know, to change it up."

Jayden wasn't alone. Alongside him, the teenage spirit kept pace. Today he wasn't scowling.

I leaned closer. Watching. Did Jayden know the spirit was there?

"No seventh grader has a chance against an eighth grader," Lily called from her end.

No, I decided. I didn't think he could see the shimmery figure in the dark hoodie and board shorts. The spirit was barefoot, I noticed. His feet only skimmed the ground.

Jayden hesitated, pushing back his thick hair with his free hand. He wasn't sure where to sit. I watched in amazement as the spirit boldly stepped forward. Gently, with a shimmery hand, he touched the shoulders of a thin boy, and the boy unknowingly edged an inch or two to the right. Then the spirit brushed up against a boy with a crew cut in a baggy sweatshirt. Crew-cut boy squirmed as if suddenly uncomfortable, then scooted to the left, to a more comfortable position.

Jayden spotted the opening and lowered himself onto the bench, unaware that it had appeared for any reason but chance.

But it wasn't by chance. The spirit made it happen. I saw.

"You sound like *you* want to be Harvest Queen, Avery," Miranda was saying across from me.

We all turned to look at Avery.

Avery blushed. "No, no, not me. I just thought it would be good if someone who was serious about it could ride on the float. Like one of us." She glanced at the poster hanging behind us. "But . . . not me."

I felt bad. Avery obviously wanted to be queen or whatever it was. I knew there was no way she would tell the other girls. They clearly thought it was silly.

I turned to look at Jayden, talking with his friends. Spirit Boy remained on watch behind him. Then I turned back to smile at Avery, to let her know I was on her side. But she was already grinning rainbows at me.

As if we shared a secret.

"Lab time, class!" Miss Klingert greeted us the next morning. "Same partners as last lab, but different tables. Check the sheet, gather your materials, and get working. Okay?"

"Okay!" we all replied. We had quickly mastered the shout-back.

I waited as Jayden moved toward the sheet with the table listings. The shimmery spirit was still by his side. I studied him. He was tall. He looked older than us. Around sixteen, I guessed.

I dug my left hand into the pocket of my cargo pants, finding the ruby crystal with my fingertips. I'd brought it to school, figuring if it was closer to Jayden it could work better. The jagged tip felt warm. Did that mean something was happening? Or was it just my body heat?

Jayden moved with the crush of bodies clamoring to see the sheet. I watched Spirit Boy step in to direct traffic. A boy who was cutting off Jayden felt a sudden need to step to the side, unknowingly redirected by Spirit Boy's guiding touch. People melted back, clearing a path—as if Jayden were a movie star or special in some way. Jayden didn't seem to notice. He reached the list without any jostling.

Was he used to obstacles being moved from his path? I wondered. Was that why he walked with such confidence?

Jayden turned and searched me out with his warm brown eyes. He raised four fingers. Table four.

I couldn't get there fast enough.

Five of us gathered at the lab table. The other team—Christine Wu and A. J. Carpenter—plus me, Jayden, and Spirit Boy.

Who is he? I was dying to know. *Why is he always next to Jayden?*

There was no one to ask.

I'd seen plenty of spirits before. Lurking in the corners of houses. Waiting at bus stops. Following me to the fudge shop on the boardwalk. I'd even spotted the not-funny gym teacher in the hallway again, though I managed to avoid him.

But I'd never seen a spirit follow one person before.

I tried not to stare, but it was hard. He scowled. His negative energy darkened the air around me. I glanced at the other three. No one else saw him. Everyone seemed bright and happy, already reading the lab instructions.

Pretend he's not here, I told myself. "What do we do?" I asked Jayden.

"We need to turn to page one forty-seven." He flipped through the book. Spirit Boy reached his hand over, and the book fell open to the correct page. Jayden began the next part of the lab, blissfully unaware that he'd had help in something as small as finding a page.

We worked together on the lab for the rest of the period, trying to understand how to measure the diameter of the sun. Spirit Boy took a step back but stayed in sight. Silently watching Jayden—and glaring at me.

"So you guys know about the Harvest Festival, right?" Christine leaned over the table, as I set up the final equation.

"Sure." Jayden examined my work. "What about it?"

"I *love* the Harvest Festival. I *love* Stellamar. And I'd really *love* to ride on the school float," Christine explained, emphasizing "love" each time. She was now so far across the table that her face hovered over our worksheet. I could smell her berry lip gloss. "So will you guys vote for me? For Harvest Queen? I'm running. Did you know?"

"No, I didn't. Sure, whatever." Jayden pointed to the sheet. "I think the decimal is in the wrong place."

He was right. I moved it.

"Sara, I know you're new and all, so you don't know me, but I'm a really great person." Her long black hair swung as she spoke. "You'll choose me too?"

"Sure," I agreed. Christine seemed nice enough. Why not?

"Excellent!" She clapped her hands together. "We're done, right?" she asked A.J.

A.J. nodded. Throughout the lab I hadn't heard him speak.

"I'm off to campaign!" She bounded over to a nearby table.

"Did your old town have this?" Jayden asked me.

"The parade-dance thing?" I shook my head. "Nothing close. It seems like it's a big deal."

"Huge. The school and the town go crazy for it." He leaned closer. "I don't know why all these clueless girls want to be the queen. It's dumb, don't you think?"

I nodded. He was so close I could smell the almond scent of the soap he'd used this morning. "Very dumb," I agreed. "Besides, this is a shore town, right? What do they harvest?"

He laughed. A low, infectious laugh. "Totally true. No farms that I know of. At least, not anymore. Maybe it's a crab harvest?"

"A seashell harvest?" I added.

"Shark harvest!"

"Are there really sharks here?"

"No. I haven't heard of any," he admitted. Still so close to me. If I lifted my hand, I could touch his cheek. "Christine would make an excellent Shark Queen." He laughed again, smiling at me.

I felt off balance, my body swaying slightly. The crystal burned through the fabric against my thigh.

Was being near Jayden making me feel this way?

My stool, I realized. It was my stool that was wobbling.

Slowly at first, then faster, tilting back and forth. I glanced down. Hands were shaking the metal legs.

I grabbed the table for support, but I wasn't fast enough. I felt myself falling . . . falling . . .

The stool clattered as it hit the floor sideways. I landed on my backside.

"Are you okay?" Jayden and A.J. both cried.

"Class," Miss Klingert said, hurrying over to me. "You need to sit squarely on these stools at all times."

"I'm fine," I said, scrambling to my feet. "I don't know what happened."

But I did.

I had seen Spirit Boy squatting down, holding the stool. Shaking it. He wanted me to fall.

And now he stood beside Jayden. Triumphant.

CHAPTER 5

"Extra help again today?" Dad asked the next morning, as he pulled up in front of the red brick middle school. "You've been going all week."

"Yes." I stared at my Converse, the ballpoint doodles I'd made on the white rubber last year already faded. I'd have to draw something new if I was going to be forever staring at my feet. That's what I did when I felt uncomfortable. And lying made me feel that way.

He lowered his aviator sunglasses and turned to me. "You know, kiddo, I'm not half bad at math. I could help."

"I know. It's just catch-up stuff. New school, new way of doing math." That so wasn't the case. I was actually ahead in math, but I didn't want to be home alone with Lady Azura after school.

I knew she wanted to talk about what I could do. What she could do. I didn't know where that conversation would lead. Would she tell my dad?

It had always been just the two of us. It wasn't easy on him, I knew. Having my mom die in childbirth. Having to raise a baby girl on his own. Whenever he held my hand, I felt his strong grip, but I knew his mind was far away, thinking about my mom. What they had. What they should have had if she hadn't died. He was here, but he wasn't. As if he were forever straddling two worlds. That was why it was important to be an easy kid, a *normal* kid, to not cause trouble. I had to keep whatever part of him I could here with me. That meant no talk of dead people.

A horn honked. The car behind us was anxious to move up in the car line.

"A kiss good-bye?" Dad asked, the skin along his blue eyes crinkling with sudden mischief. He leaned in.

"Not here," I protested, gathering my bulging book bag. The sidewalk was filled with kids in my classes.

"Too cool for Dad." He pretended to pout. "Okay, but I'm claiming my kiss tonight."

"Deal." I scrambled out of the car and headed into the school.

Goose bumps rose on my bare arms as I opened my locker door. Once again I was greeted with the unexplainable chill. I unloaded the binders from my bag and tucked my brown-bag lunch into my own private refrigerator. Where was the coldness coming from? I searched the metallic locker once again for a vent or a fan or something.

Brushing across the top shelf, my fingers stopped at an unfamiliar object. Carefully I pulled it out.

A crown. A small paper crown.

I examined the shiny gold paper. Pointy zigzags cut with scissors and trimmed with gold glitter. A tiny piece of clear tape holding it together, as if a child had created it.

Standing on my toes, I inspected the single shelf for a note. Nothing.

Who put this here? I looked closer at the paper crown. No writing anywhere.

Did Lily do this? Maybe her four-year-old sister Cammie had made it. But why give it to me with no note?

I found Lily before lunch kneeling at her locker, sorting through papers.

"Thanks for the gifts."

"What gifts?" She didn't look up. She was searching for something.

"The flower. This crown." I reached out my hand. The gold crown rested on my palm.

Lily gazed at me, scrunching her nose. "I didn't give you that. Or a flower."

"Really? But they were in my locker."

"I don't have your combo," she pointed out. She pulled a piece of paper from her pile. "I need to hand this in next period." She pushed the mess of papers into her locker, slamming the door. As we walked toward the cafeteria, she reached for the paper crown. "It's pretty."

My mind was still puzzling over what she'd said. Who had my locker combination? No one, as far as I knew. "There was a pink flower, too. I don't know why they were there."

"Oh!" Lily stopped short at the cafeteria's opened double doors. Her eyes wide with excitement, she bounced on her toes. "You have a secret admirer!"

"A what? No way. I don't even know anyone," I scoffed.

"But someone knows you," Lily replied in a singsong voice.

She spent the entire lunch period debating the potential of every boy as my gift-giving admirer. Each choice seemed more ridiculous than the next.

"Tamara sits next to Luke Goldberg in English, and she says he asked about you," Lily reported. "I bet it's him." She gestured in the direction of a sandy-haired boy I didn't know but who I'd noticed smiling at me in the social studies class we had together.

"He's never even spoken to me," I protested.

"Actions speak louder than words, my mom always says," Lily replied knowingly.

I looked at Luke, but my gaze traveled to the end of his table, where Jayden sat. He tossed a piece of popcorn in the air and caught it in his mouth. Raising his fist in victory, he smiled, and I found myself wishing it were him. Maybe he'd left me the gifts.

Another popcorn piece launched into the air. The outline of a shimmering hand reached out and guided the kernel into Jayden's open mouth. Victory again.

Jayden celebrated, as Spirit Boy hovered beside him. Then his translucent companion turned and caught me watching. He directed a dark glare my way. Warning me away.

I sighed. It couldn't be Jayden, I realized. Spirit Boy would never allow it. Would he?

"Toss your trash and come with me," Lily whispered five minutes before lunch ended.

"Where?"

She nudged me. "Just come."

I crumpled my paper bag, folded the paper crown, and stood. I could make out the gym teacher across the room, pushing the trash can closer so a girl with bad aim aced the slam dunk of her apple core. I led Lily to a different can.

"I want to see who signed up to run for Harvest Queen," she confided, as I followed her down the narrow aisles and around the crowded tables. "The list is over there."

"I thought you said it was silly."

"It is." Lily stopped before a piece of notebook paper stapled to a neon-orange poster board on the wall. "Did I tell you I joined the school newspaper? I'm going to be a reporter. This is news, so I need to know about it. It's like my job now."

She may be a reporter, I thought, *but Lily's genuinely curious.* But after putting down Harvest Queen to Miranda, she couldn't tell the girls at our table she was dying to know who was on the list.

"Caroline Melillo . . . Dina Martino . . . Chloe Wohl, she's nice . . ." She read the names out loud. I leaned in. It was hard to hear over the chatter and squeals of the entire seventh grade.

"Ava Gomez . . . all eighth graders . . . oh, Christine Wu, she's in seventh, and—" Lily stopped reading. Her brow furrowed, and she tilted her head. "I didn't know you wanted to be Harvest Queen."

"What? I don't."

"You could have told me, you know." She sounded hurt.

"What are you talking about?" I demanded.

She pointed to the final name on the list: Sara Collins.

"That's not me," I said.

"Oh, come on, Sara. If you wanted to run, you should have just told me—"

"I didn't sign up," I insisted, still staring at my name written on the sheet.

"Really?" Lily sounded dubious.

"Really. Someone is playing a mean joke." I grabbed the black Sharpie hanging on a string by the poster board and blacked out my name.

"That's so weird," Lily said.

I glanced at the gym teacher, over at Jayden and the Spirit Boy, then down at the folded paper crown in my hand. Lily didn't know the half of it.

I doodled on my sneakers, swirls spiraling along the tongue. Every few seconds I stole secretive glances at Jayden, sitting on a stool to my right. First period. Science. Jayden. He'd said hi but then started talking to A.J. about a video game with different levels. Spirit Boy hovered in the corner, disinterested.

No new gifts in my locker this morning. I wondered again if there was any chance Jayden had given me the flower. I thought back to Lady Azura reading my palm. She said I'd *meet* a tall, dark stranger. She didn't say he'd *like* me. But then in my vision he'd looked at me like he really did like me. A lot.

I wasn't sure what it all meant.

"Announcements, class," Miss Klingert called out. "Eyes on the screen." During class, the huge white screen displayed her PowerPoint presentations, but in the morning, schoolwide announcements were broadcast over it. Kids in the journalism club took turns as on-air anchors. Usually it was mind-numbingly boring. Jayden and A.J. continued debating the best way to reach level five.

I barely listened to the rundown of after-school activities. I had to go right home. I'd promised Dad. It had been days since I'd seen Lady Azura alone. Luckily, she never emerged from her rooms before noon. She said it took time to "put on her face." So avoiding her in the morning was easy. Then, by dinnertime, Dad was around. I spent my nights hidden upstairs doing homework and messing on the computer with the photographs I'd taken this summer.

Sports scores passed in a blur, though from his reaction I guessed that Jayden was on the soccer team. They won, I think.

Harvest Queen candidates were next. Eighth-grade girls I didn't know. Their school photos flashed on the screen as each name was announced.

My mind drifted back to Jayden. Maybe I should go watch him play soccer.

"That's me!" Christine shrieked across from me. I glanced up at the screen and caught a stiff studio portrait of Christine smiling widely. Kids in class cheered for her.

Maybe I could join the school website as a sports photographer, I thought. I liked to take pictures, and then I'd have a reason to hang out at the soccer games—

I sensed the quiet immediately. All the kids stopped talking among themselves, as if on cue.

I gazed up. Dozens of eyes stared at me.

Jayden, A.J., and Christine stared at me. Then at the screen.

Me—on the screen.

A hastily shot, blurred image of me walking down the hall was being shown on every screen in every classroom in the school!

And then my name. Out loud. Announced on the morning broadcast.

Sara Collins. For Harvest Queen.

CHAPTER 6

"Seriously?" Christine leaned over the table in disbelief. "Seriously?"

"That's cool," A.J. murmured.

"Who is she?" asked someone behind me.

"The new girl. Over there. See?" Stools scraped. Kids looked.

"Can you believe it?" someone else said. "She's new. No one even knows her."

I couldn't believe it. I had crossed off my name. I hadn't written it there in the first place, but I had crossed it off. Why were they announcing it now to the whole school? I cringed. The whole school!

"You're really going after Harvest Queen?" Christine's voice was measured, trying to hide her annoyance.

"No." I shook my head wildly. "It's a mistake."

"Well, then you should tell someone. Go to the office," Christine said. "You've got to fix it."

She was right. I raised my hand.

"Yes?" Miss Klingert was already putting up a PowerPoint about sunspots.

"May I have a pass? To the office. Please?"

She turned, noticing me for the first time since school began. "Is it important? Can it wait until the end of class?"

I hesitated, but Christine mouthed, *Now*.

"May I go now?" I asked.

Miss Klingert handed me a pass, and I hurried out of the room and down the empty hall in the direction of the office.

"Hey, Sara!" Avery emerged from the girls' bathroom. She'd been folding her yellow pass into what looked like an origami bird. "Aren't you excited about Harvest Queen?"

I was having trouble processing all this information. I didn't know what to say.

"It's about time someone ran who—"

"I'm not running."

Avery smirked. "Of course you are. You were announced."

"That doesn't mean anything."

"But they said it." Her face brightened. "Hey, don't worry, I have it all figured out. I can help you."

"Help me what?" The office door beckoned, wide open, down the long hallway. *I have to get there,* I thought.

"Campaign. Get votes. I've been waiting for this, to—"

"Thanks," I cut her off. "It's a mistake, though, and I need to fix it." I moved toward the open door, then felt bad about brushing her off. "See you at lunch," I called over my shoulder.

The office hummed with activity. Two assistants typed furiously, one muttering to herself. Several teachers milled about, placing absent students' work into folders and drinking coffee out of mugs adorned with apples and pencils and other teacherlike artwork. A parent stood at the counter, pushing her child's clarinet case toward a gray-haired woman, reminding her that Greg had band second period.

I waited until the mother left, then stepped up

to the counter. I told the woman, who seemed as if she ran the office, that they'd announced my name by mistake this morning. She frowned. Then she shuffled toward a desk behind her. She returned with the piece of notebook paper and some other sheets.

"Is this your name?" she asked. She pointed to *Sara Collins* written in blue pen immediately below the black marker cross-out on the sign-up sheet.

"Yes . . . but no!" I took a deep breath, trying to string words together. "I mean, that is my name, but I didn't sign up."

She heaved a sigh. "But you filled out the permission form." She laid another sheet on top of the sign-up list.

I gaped. A two-page form with my name on it, completely filled out in the same blue ink. I held the paper close, my hands shaking. It was my handwriting. *My handwriting!* My loopy *L*s. My words slanting to the left.

"The form came with rules. You checked off that you understood the rules, and your parent signed." She pointed to the signature on the second page.

"I didn't fill out this form," I insisted, my voice a panicked whisper.

"This is not your writing?" She furrowed her brow.

"It is, but . . ." I didn't know. Who would do this? Who copied my handwriting so well? And forged my dad's signature? *Who?*

"Are you okay, dear?" Her tone changed to one of concern.

"Yes. No. I need to get out of this. . . ."

She nodded. "I can't do that for you. Since we do have a form you filled out with your parent's permission, the principal needs to review this. Unfortunately, Principal Bowman is at an off-site meeting today. You'll have to stop by on Monday."

"But I don't want to be on the Harvest Queen list—"

"I can't change anything until the principal returns to assess the situation. Do you need a pass back to class?"

"But—"

She shrugged. "That's all I can do." She handed me a yellow pass. "Others are waiting." She indicated the line of kids forming behind me.

I left the office just as the bell ending first period sounded. In seconds, the hall filled with kids. I stood for a moment, still puzzled about my handwriting on that form. Then, over the noise of squeaking sneakers and voices raised in greeting, I heard a familiar deep laugh.

The shimmery form of the gym teacher stood across the hall, holding his belly and laughing.

At me.

"Surprise," Dad called that afternoon, when I climbed the narrow stairs to the second floor. He sat in front of his laptop at the wide wooden table we'd brought from California. In the small kitchen in our old house, the table had seemed comically large. Every night when I was little, and even when I'd outgrown it, we'd set six places at the table—two for me and Dad, the other four for my stuffed animals. We always had "guests."

Today the table looked small and adrift in the high-ceilinged main room of the rambling Victorian house. We didn't own enough furniture to fill this room, let alone the six other rooms that made up the top two floors that we rented.

"You're home!" I gave him a big hug.

No one-on-one with Lady Azura today, I realized.

"Yep, kiddo, I snuck out early 'cause it's Friday,"

he said. "My boss thinks I'm still at a site writing up a jewelry theft report." He shrugged. "The wonders of a laptop."

He worked as an insurance claims adjuster. If someone had a fire or a car crash, my dad was the one who decided how much of the repair the insurance company should pay. I sank into the chair next to him, digging my hand into his opened bag of pretzels.

"How was school?"

"Fine." My autopilot response.

He stopped typing. "I don't believe you."

I shrugged. How could I explain? "It's just . . . weird."

"All new things are weird. Give it another week or two, and what seems weird now will be completely normal," he said.

I doubted that. I picked flecks of salt, one by one, off a pretzel. I wondered how much I could safely tell him. "It's confusing here."

"The schoolwork?"

I shook my head. "I'm good with the school stuff. It's the people—and the way things happen."

I could see the uncertainty in his blue eyes. "The

ice cream place on the boardwalk hasn't closed yet for the season. Double-fudge crunch?"

Ice cream was always one of Dad's answers.

Ice cream wasn't going to make the spirits in the school go away or explain who signed me up for Harvest Queen, but I knew it was the best he could do.

"Let's go," I said, standing.

I pulled my comforter to my chin, my eyes open. My body stiffened as I listened to the house. Creaking floorboards. Clanging pipes.

Old house noises, I lied to myself.

But it wasn't the house. It was the mustached man who paced the floors of our main room. His heavy shoes slapped the floor in an agitated rhythm. It was the wooden rocking chair squeaking in the pink bedroom down the hall. The woman's painful wails of despair as she rocked and cried. Cried and rocked. The faint odor of pipe smoke drifted through the vents from the man in the sailor cap, forever perched at the upstairs window.

The house was alive, even at night. Alive with dead people.

I had learned to sleep through it. I ignored them. They ignored me.

But tonight I was wide awake. The glowing numbers on the alarm clock taunted me. 1:36. 1:37.

I closed my eyes. Images flickered on the back of my lids. The teenage spirit, his hoodie drawn over his head, glaring at me. The gym teacher's belly shaking as his laughter echoed through the halls. My name being called over and over again on the loudspeaker. Everyone staring.

Then the singing started. A high-pitched melody. I opened my eyes and strained my ears. A noise I'd never heard before.

Off-key. Faint words about a chickadee and a woman lost.

A spirit in the house? I didn't know. Had the Sad Woman started singing?

I listened, catching a few words but not all. The song repeated several times, and I found myself humming along. I pushed back my comforter and swung my legs aside. My bare feet touched the cold floor. Where was the song coming from?

Awake and curious, I padded down the dark hall.

The low rumblings of snores outside my father's door told me he was asleep. I tiptoed into our main room. In the shadows I could make out the mustached guy, pacing in front of our worn corduroy sofa. He didn't stop for me. I paused. The song continued softly. A woman's voice, struggling for the high notes.

I gripped the banister at the top of the stairs. What was I doing? I didn't know what kind of spirits haunted this house. I should run back to my bed. Hide.

The melody floated up. The song beckoning me down the stairs.

One step at a time.

Closer to the music.

My feet seemed to move on their own.

Shadows flickered on the foyer walls. Shivering in my tank top and thin pajama boxers, I crossed my arms over my chest and rubbed my arms. The chorus about the chickadee lilted in from the kitchen.

Don't go, I told myself.

But I couldn't stop. My feet moved me forward into the dark kitchen.

CHAPTER 7

I hesitated in the doorway, too frightened to breathe. A figure floated in the shadows. All in white from head to toe.

The melody was softer now. A gentle hum. The figure swayed in time with the song. I pressed my fingernails into my palms as the ghostly figure moved toward me. I gaped at the thin outstretched arms. At the blue-white skin. At the two steaming mugs.

"Marshmallows or whipped cream?" the raspy voice inquired.

I'd lost all ability to speak.

"Both then?" The figure placed the mugs on the table. Two napkins, two spoons, and two plates of gingersnaps already waited on the pale pink tablecloth. "I was expecting you."

"You were?" I croaked. My mind slowly put together the pieces. Not a spirit. It was Lady Azura dressed in a long, white satin bathrobe. A white silk scarf wrapped like a turban concealed her mahogany-dyed hair. Her face, stripped bare of its usual makeup, was colorless in the dim light from over the stove. Her wrinkled skin hugged her high cheekbones like crepe paper.

"Some nights are not meant for sleep. Some are meant for midnight snacks. Sit." She pointed to a chair, then slid into the one opposite.

For several minutes I concentrated on blowing the steam from my drink. Lady Azura nibbled a cookie, watching and waiting for me to speak. But what could I say? *I see dead people, do you?* I didn't think my mouth could form those words.

I glanced at the ceiling, noticing that the mustached man's constant footsteps had now stopped. *Tap, tap, tap.* He drummed his thick-soled shoe impatiently, no longer pacing. A minute later he resumed his measured steps.

"Some nights I find the rhythm soothing." Lady Azura waved toward the ceiling. "Other nights I want to whack the poor man in the knee and put him and me out of our misery." Her lips turned up in a smile.

"You hear them too?" My voice came out in a whisper.

"Yes." Lady Azura met my questioning gaze straight on. "Mr. Broadhurst has a lot on his mind. He runs a large printing company. Or used to back in 1895."

"Can you see them?" My hands trembled, and I shoved them in my lap. *I'm not the only one!* The words repeated like a chant in my head.

"Some I see. Some I used to and don't anymore." She shrugged. "Maybe they left, though I suspect my ability isn't what it used to be. The older I get, the more out of touch I am."

I suddenly needed her to say it. Admit it straight out. "They're dead, right? The other people in this house."

She smiled knowingly. "Yes, Sara, they are no longer living. They are spirits. You and I are some of the special ones who can see them."

"And hear them talk?" I wanted to get it all out there.

"And hear them. Though, I admit, my hearing spirits days may be behind me now. Been kind of fuzzy on that the last few years. I can still call up spirits. Of course, who shows up is not always who was on the guest list." Her expression grew serious. "My little communication problem is our secret. I have a business to run. Understood?"

I nodded. "So it's for real? You can do everything your sign says?"

"Yes and no." She sipped her hot chocolate. "Who is to know what is real and what isn't? I can't say. Can you? What appears to be a snake in a darkened room is revealed to be a rope when the light is thrown on. But if the light is never turned on, it will be forever a snake in our minds."

"I don't understand." Again with the riddles.

"There are many kinds of real. Are the spirits you see real?"

"Yes. Well, to me. But others can't see them," I fumbled to explain.

"Different realities." She pushed a marshmallow under the hot chocolate, then watched it bob to the surface. "Many people will say what you experience is not real because they themselves have not experienced it. They can accept only what they can prove, given the five senses they have."

"I used to think I was crazy," I admitted, "because I see people everyone else doesn't."

"Not everyone." She readjusted her robe and leaned forward. "I see them. Others see them. Not many others. I have known only a handful in my life."

I'm not the only one. I'm not the only one. The words chorused around me.

"Why me?" I had so many questions. "Why can I see them and not my dad or Lily?"

"You have an ability . . . a power . . . a sense that is sharper than the five senses." Her eyes moved around the dim kitchen, searching for a way to explain. She walked to the cluttered desk. "This is my cell phone." She held up a small black phone.

"Yours?" I couldn't believe someone so old had a cell.

"Yes, mine." She grinned. "I thought I'd use something you'd recognize. Try thinking of people as cell phones. Some are not in tune with the world around them. They function on just one bar of power. Others are highly sensitive to smells or tastes or sounds. They work with three, four, or five bars on any given day. But Sara, you have many more bars than the screen will ever show. You can receive information from beyond the scope of the phone's range. You are wired differently. Better, I think."

"And you, too?"

"Me, too, though I suspect your powers are stronger than mine. You saw and heard Lily's great-aunt. I did not."

"I never used to." Again I fumbled to explain. "They've always been there. Spirits, I mean. When I was little, teachers and babysitters thought I had imaginary friends." I let out the breath I'd been holding. Talking about this made my throat tighten.

"Your father . . ." For the first time, Lady Azura looked uneasy. "Does he know?"

"No," I said quickly. "He'd be freaked out. He refuses to even watch a TV show that has a supernatural plot. You won't tell him, will you?" I could hear my desperation.

"No, I won't tell him," she said softly. "But Sara, you shouldn't shut him out. He may understand more than you think."

"He wouldn't," I insisted. She knew nothing of my dad's and my relationship.

"Coming here may have changed the way he thinks."

"You're wrong. We can't tell him. Ever." I thought for a moment about Lady Azura's big, old house and the spirits lurking in almost every room. "When I moved here, I suddenly saw them everywhere. And clearer. I could hear them too."

Lady Azura's dark eyes sparkled. "I believe you are feeding off my energy." She raised her arms and clasped her hands in front of her. "The potential! Oh, the potential is huge!"

"For what?" The fluttery, panicked feeling rose from my stomach into my throat.

"My powers have weakened with age, but you are just beginning. You have the ability to siphon my heightened energies and use them to connect with the unconnected. There is no telling what you can do."

She must have noticed the terrified look on my face, so she added, "Sara, you have a gift. It is a good thing."

"It doesn't feel that way. I don't know how to work it, and I don't know what these spirits want from me or how to get them to leave me alone." I gnawed my bottom lip so hard I tasted blood. "I don't want this. I just want to be normal."

"Normal is overrated, my child." Lady Azura leaned forward as if to touch me, but I shrank back. "You are special. Very few are. Be proud. I am."

"So there's no way to make it go away? To make *them* go away?" I couldn't believe this. I thought she'd have the solution. The way to fix this problem. But she didn't see it as a problem. She was proud she could see spirits.

"They never go away," she said softly. "But there are ways to control them. Ways for you to be in charge. You still have a lot to learn."

The hot chocolate left a bitter aftertaste in my mouth. I swallowed hard and stood. "I don't want to learn!" I realized I was shouting and lowered my voice. I couldn't wake my dad. "I don't want ghosts in my house or in my school!"

"There are forces, Sara, that are greater than what we want. Let me help you—"

"I can't do this." I was suddenly exhausted. "I'm—I'm sorry." I hurried out of the kitchen and padded back up the stairs.

I'm not the only one.

So what? I didn't want to be in a special club with Lady Azura. I just wanted to be like everyone else.

Was that so wrong?

CHAPTER 8

Principal Bowman was absent on Monday. Absent! I didn't think principals could be absent. Didn't she know kids needed her?

I'd spent all weekend planning what I'd say. How I'd stand up for myself and fix everything. I didn't need Lady Azura's help. I could at least get out of the Harvest Queen mix-up by myself.

But not with the principal gone.

I slipped into science, flashing Miss Klingert my pass. No labs today. She diagramed eclipses, and we took notes. Jayden buried his head in his notebook. He never looked at me. Not once.

Other kids did. Ever since I'd entered the building, strange eyes watched me.

Christine caught up with me as soon as the bell rang.

"So you fixed it, right?" she asked.

"Kind of." I balanced my notebooks in my arms and watched Jayden head toward the door. Spirit Boy followed. Jayden stopped and looked back at me and Christine. He shook his head and plunged into the hallway crowds. Should I run after him, tell him I wasn't the dance queen type, that it was a mistake—

"What do you mean? Are you in or out?" Christine demanded.

"I still need to talk to the principal."

"You're playing me, right?" She had her hands on her hips. "Just own up that you're totally running against me. I trusted you and you lied to me."

"I didn't lie. You've got to believe me. I'll be out of it tomorrow," I promised.

"You won't win," she pointed out. "No one knows who you are."

As I squeezed my way through the halls to my locker, I realized Christine was wrong. Kids did know who I was. I could hear them whispering. *New girl.*

"Do you like them?" Avery waited beside my locker.

"What?" I snapped. I was in a bad mood.

"The posters. I made three this weekend, but if I

can get Tamara and Lily to help, we can make a lot tonight. Miranda might not be so into it, but I'll ask her, too." She pointed across the hall.

A huge poster proclaiming SURF A NEW WAVE FOR HARVEST QUEEN! SARA COLLINS! hung on the wall. She had drawn a surfboard in jewel-tone markers and decorated it with little crowns all covered in gold glitter.

I wanted to tear it down. It made no sense. I didn't surf. And I wasn't running! But then I saw how excited Avery was. I couldn't be mean to her. She was trying to be my friend.

"Wow!" I faked enthusiasm. "I can't believe you did that."

"I know, right? I told you I'd be the best campaign manager. I have so many ideas. I'm so glad you're doing this." She bounced on her toes. She stood a full head shorter than I did, yet she seemed to be everywhere at once, her energy filling the halls.

"The thing is, I'm not doing it," I admitted. "I'm still waiting to see the principal. I'm sorry you did all that work."

"But Sara, you have to. We need to put the others

in their place. You and me. I'll be behind the scenes, and you'll wear the crown." She pointed to one of the glitter crowns on her poster.

I suddenly had the strangest feeling. The crowns she'd drawn looked exactly like the crown I'd found in my locker.

I examined the poster again. Avery was very artistic. Even though I didn't like the message, the hand lettering was excellent. Had Avery written my name on the application? Had she left the crown in my locker? Was she the one behind all this?

She tapped my locker with her hand. "Don't drop out, okay?" Then she walked away.

For once, the icy air felt good.

I stood in front of my open locker, letting the coldness wash over me.

What did I know about Avery? She'd been friends with Lily since third grade. She was very into gymnastics and could do something called a back tuck. She'd always been nice to me, although she was kind of intense at times. She had this way of staring at you when she thought you weren't looking. From talk at the lunchroom table, I gathered that she was passionate about lots of causes. Lily told me that Avery headed up every canned food drive at school.

Not much to go on.

The hall was emptying out. Only a few stragglers remained, taking their time before strolling to class. Math. I had math next. I bent down to grab my blue binder.

"Interesting locker decoration," commented a deep voice behind me.

I whirled around. Gym teacher. Grinning as if he'd heard the funniest joke.

"What?" I couldn't believe how real he seemed. How solid. His bulbous nose. The wiry hairs in his thick eyebrows.

He nodded at the inside of my locker door. A piece of paper was tucked under the square mirror I'd attached. I gulped and reached for it. The thick paper felt dry and brittle between my fingertips.

CELEBRATE STELLAMAR

AT THE HARVEST FESTIVAL.

PARADE AT NOON.

SEPTEMBER 27, 1952

Simple block letters. The background had panels of faded red, orange, and yellow. A white trim bordered the flyer.

"I didn't figure you for an oldies kind of girl," the gym teacher cracked. "Me on the other hand, I love oldies! I'm so old, I'm not over the hill, I'm over the mountain!" He broke into a deep guffaw, holding his shaking belly. "Get it?"

The final bell rang.

"Don't want to be late." He produced a packet of detention slips from his tracksuit pocket. "Not to worry. The early bird catches the worm, but the second mouse eats the cheese!" He laughed again. A hollow, empty laugh. His body shimmered, then faded.

I slipped the old flyer into my binder, slammed my locker shut, and raced to math class, the gym teacher's laughter ringing in my ears.

I followed Lily into the lunch line. I usually bring my lunch, but I needed to talk where the other girls couldn't hear.

"It's so not fair." I told her about Principal Bowman taking the day off.

"You'll get out of it, don't worry. And if you don't, my cousin Dawn Marie can lend you her Harvest Queen dress. It's bubblegum pink with tons of ruffles and all this scratchy lace. You'll look so . . . royal!" She giggled and nudged me with her elbow, nearly knocking her iced tea bottle off her tray.

"Quit it!" I nudged her back. "Tell Dawn Marie to keep her dress." I watched her grab a plastic-wrapped bagel with cream cheese. "Or maybe Avery should wear it. She seems to be the most into it, don't you think?"

"Totally," Lily agreed. "Avery's all over it. Did you see the posters she made? They're actually really cool. I mean, if you were really running"—she noticed my exasperated look—"which you are not."

"Do you think Avery seems more than just interested? Like she wanted this to happen?"

"She loves the attention. Actually, if you did run, Avery really could help. She comes up with the best schemes. There was this one time when we were selling Girl Scout cookies . . ." I tuned Lily out as I picked up on a conversation farther down the line.

"That's her. Sara Collins," one girl said, pointing in my direction.

I stared at the selection of chips in front of me. Sweet potato, nacho, cheddar. I didn't dare turn.

"She's not part of that snotty Caroline-Dina group, right? She's new, and she's really doing this?" the other girl asked.

"Yeah. Didn't you read Katherine's blog this morning? She called her the normal-girl candidate. She's not part of any group. Not a jock or a fashionista or a drama diva or an all-As-all-the-timer. She's like a regular girl, like us. Normal."

"You don't know that," the second girl said.

"I hope so." The first girl sounded so wistful. "Don't you?"

"Sara?" Lily elbowed my arm. "You coming to the table?"

She'd already paid. I was dying to look back at the girls, but I couldn't face them. They thought I was normal. *Me!*

The weight of it was too much. I couldn't have these girls depending on me to change the clique structure of this school.

By the end of my last-period class, I decided to confront Avery. It was the only way. She walked home too, but in the other direction. I'd just get to the door first and . . . I didn't know what. But I had to say something. If she'd gotten me into this, then she could help me get out of it.

I steadied myself for the arctic blast.

It didn't seem as cold, I'd found, if I psyched myself up before opening my locker. I'd grab my book bag and run to intercept Avery. I could even walk with her partway, since Lily had left early for a dentist appointment.

I balanced my three binders and textbook in one arm, then twirled the combination lock, clicked it into place, and pulled open the door.

My eyes watered slightly with the sudden chill.

I pushed the door with my foot—and caught sight of my reflection in the mirror.

I gasped, unable to turn away from what stared back.

My binders clattered to the floor, metal rings popping and papers scattering. My hands flew up to cover my mouth.

To cover my scream.

CHAPTER 9

A crown.

A crudely drawn crown on my locker mirror.

Drawn with pink lipstick.

My legs trembled as I stared at it.

Someone had been sneaking into my locker.

Leaving weird messages that made no sense. What did the crown mean? Run for Harvest Queen? Or was it a warning *not* to?

Was it Avery or someone else?

I wrapped my arms around my ribs, pulling into myself. Everything was wrong.

"Locker explosion?"

He appeared beside me, his dark eyes surveying the damage. For a moment, all I could do was stare. The way his brown hair swept over his broad forehead. The woven band of hemp on his wrist. Then I noticed the papers. Everywhere. My homework. My class notes. Scattered on the floor.

Jayden bent down and began to gather them. "The lockers are wired like time bombs. I think the principal does it. A sinister plot to freak out kids," he joked.

I smiled. How could I not? "Thanks." I quickly began to scoop up my papers. "It wasn't a terrorist plot. The mirror scared me."

"Bad hair day?" Jayden asked. "That could definitely lead a Harvest Queen to destroy school property."

"No." I stood and pointed to the mirror.

To the mirror that was now empty. No crown. No anything.

"What?" he asked, standing.

I stared at the blank mirror. I had seen a crown—right?

Suddenly I wasn't so sure.

"Uh . . . nothing." I couldn't stop looking at the mirror. At my quizzical expression staring back at me.

"Here's your book." He pushed my textbook toward me, and I slowly reached for it. Then stopped. Midair.

We had done this before.

He had been standing like this, leaning against the locker and handing me a book. And now . . . here . . . again.

My vision. This was it!

"Do you want it?" He waved the book.

I grabbed hold of the spine, then stepped closer. He smelled just right. Almond soap and peanut butter. I inhaled and took another step closer. The ruby crystal, tucked today in my back pocket, was working. Bringing us together.

The hall grew dark. The air heavy. As if a storm was brewing.

He was here.

Spirit Boy. He stood beside Jayden. Watching me. Daring me with his cold eyes to draw closer.

Jayden must have sensed something too, because he edged away from me. He scanned the nearly empty halls. "Wow! I'm going to miss my bus!" He ran for the main door, his athletic stride covering the distance with ease. Spirit Boy kept pace. "Later!" Jayden called to me down the hall.

"I don't want to be Harvest Queen!" I yelled after him. But it was too late. He'd already gone.

"This is a first." Principal Bowman pushed her tortoiseshell frames higher onto the bridge of her nose the next afternoon. "Girls usually beg me to let them run for Harvest Queen, but you want out."

"I do." I squirmed as the chair's metal slats stuck to my jeans. The temperature had climbed to the nineties even though it was mid-September. An unexpected heat wave. Stale, moist air clung to everything in her office, despite the open window behind her desk.

"What changed your mind?" She pushed her damp hair back from her face. Small curls remained plastered to her full cheeks.

"I didn't change my mind." I explained again how I hadn't signed up. That someone was playing a joke on me.

"A mighty elaborate joke." She squinted her eyes behind the lenses, trying to figure me out.

"Can you take my name off the list? Please?" It didn't seem like a lot to ask. "All those other girls want it. You don't need me."

"I could, but—" She paused, folding a piece of

paper into accordion pleats. "I think that you should stay in the race."

"What?" I blurted.

"You're new. It's not easy to meet people. Think of this as an opportunity. A happy accident." She fanned herself with her pleated paper fan. "You can get involved in the school and make friends at the same time."

For real? When was the last time she was in middle school? Had things really changed that much in thirty years? Didn't she know that no one would vote for me?

I would be a joke. A huge joke.

One of the secretaries pushed opened the office door before I could protest. "You're backing up out here. Two parents, three disciplinaries, and the computers in the eighth-grade wing are off-line again."

"We're almost done, Esther." With a sigh, the principal placed her fan down on the dark-wood credenza behind her, next to a ceramic vase filled with orange marigolds. She turned to me. "Are we good?"

Stand up for yourself, I silently commanded. *Do something.* "I don't want to do it, and I don't think I should be forced to."

"No one's forcing anything, Sara." She sighed again, gazing out the door at the crowd of overheated disgruntled parents and belligerent students. "Look, if you really don't want—"

My left foot began to tingle. Pinpricks ran along the sole and up to my ankle.

At that moment, a breeze materialized for the first time all day. Air swept through the office from the open window.

And in the breeze, the outline of hands.

Faint, shimmery hands.

Reaching out.

The prickling climbed my legs. The signal I knew all too well.

The hands. The cool air. They swirled into one, knocking the vase of flowers over with unexpected force. Petals and stems scattered on the floor. Water flooded over the wooden credenza, soaking papers and files.

"Oh, my!" Principal Bowman leaped to her feet and frantically gathered the paper in the path of the water. "This is the strangest weather. I wonder if a storm is coming."

Tingling coursed through my entire body. I sat frozen, unable to get up to help. I could only stare at the vase, lying on its side. A sudden breeze hadn't blown it over. There had been hands. Hands pushing it.

"Esther? Can you get me some paper towels?" Principal Bowman bellowed. "Oh no, the school board minutes are soaked. Look, uh . . ." For a moment she seemed to forget who I was. "Sara. Sleep on it tonight. Think about it. We'll talk again tomorrow."

"But—"

Esther hurried in with a handful of towels, and together they squatted below the desk to repair the damage.

"You can take a pass from the office counter," Esther called up to me. "Seventh-grade lunch is about to start."

"Tomorrow," Principal Bowman instructed. "Think about it."

I left with the events playing over and over like a YouTube video in my mind.

That wasn't a weird act of Mother Nature.

A spirit had knocked over the vase.

On purpose.

To cause a distraction.

To make me run for Harvest Queen.

A huge, glittery poster with my name on it hung behind me. I couldn't see it, but I knew with every bite of my turkey sandwich that it was there. Avery had been hard at work. I was surprised she hadn't erected a billboard on the boardwalk.

Maybe tomorrow.

"Avery, it's really nice of you. Really nice, but—" She'd left before I could talk to her yesterday. "I told you I'm getting out of it."

"But everyone thinks it's so cool that you're doing it," she said.

"I don't think it's cool," Miranda muttered. I heard, but didn't say anything. Miranda was the only one of the group who didn't like me. I didn't think she hated me, though. I didn't know. I couldn't figure her out.

"Sara's being in the race has really shaken things up." Avery grinned in high-def color. Totally excited.

She reminded me of Stewy, my aunt Charlotte's beagle. Every day, Stewy chases the squirrels in their yard. He never catches them. He never has the slightest chance of catching them. But he keeps at it, completely oblivious that all his effort is completely wasted.

"Aves, what kind of paint did you use?" Tamara asked.

Avery shrugged. "The normal kind. Why?"

Tamara cocked her head, examining the posters throughout the cafeteria. "I don't know. There's something about your posters. Makes you want to look at them. A lot."

"I see it too!" Lily nodded. "They kind of sparkle, like they're lit up from behind."

I noticed it too. A shimmer. A special gleam. Avery's posters popped. They pulled you in.

I ran my top teeth over the chapped skin on my lip. Maybe I was wrong. Maybe Avery *wasn't* behind all this. I thought about the hands. The aura coming off the posters . . . maybe it was supernatural.

A spirit.

I watched the gym teacher. His body was so faint today. He blew a whistle at a table of boys throwing pretzel sticks. But they didn't stop. Why would they? They couldn't hear him.

Was *he* the one?

"Sara, scoot down," Lily whispered. She sat to my right. "Quickly!"

I scooted. "Why?"

"Jack, Luke, Jayden, Garrett, and the other Jack are coming over." She straightened the three tank tops she wore layered.

Tamara, Avery, Miranda, and Lily joked and talked with the boys as if they'd all known one another forever.

I reached into my brown paper bag and pulled out a chocolate pudding cup and a plastic spoon. Lady Azura had a thing for pudding cups. Our fridge was stocked with them. As I rolled back the foil top, my eyes drifted to the gym teacher patrolling the aisles. Kids threw things. They shoved one another. He tried to control them, stop them, but couldn't.

As his anger mounted, his body grew fainter.

In and out, his image flickered. A thermometer of his emotions.

"Hey. Pudding cup, huh?" Jayden was suddenly sitting to my right. How did that happen? Lily was now across the table. Lily and Avery talked to the boys about the Harvest Festival, making plans for us all to meet up at the parade.

"Have you ever had chocomole?" Jayden asked.

"Chocomole? What's that?"

He leaned across me, the sleeve of his white T-shirt brushing the underside of my chin. I breathed in the familiar smell of him. "Aves, are you done with those?" he asked.

"Sure." Avery pushed her half-eaten bag of potato chips toward him.

"Excellent." The bag crinkled as Jayden pulled back. He produced a chip and plunged it into the pudding. "You've had guacamole, right? Well, this is chocomole. It works better with tortilla chips. These are a little flimsy." He held out the pudding-covered chip.

"That looks gross!"

"Come on . . . try it. Or do Harvest Queens only eat healthy foods?"

"I'm not a Harvest Queen!"

"That's what you say. But I don't believe you. I see posters." He waved the chip, and splotches of pudding dripped onto the table. Then, grinning, he popped it into his mouth.

"Not my doing," I insisted. "It's all a mistake."

"Interesting." He pretended to think about it.

We were still sitting at a table filled with kids in an enormous room filled with even more kids, yet in an odd way it seemed like we were alone. I felt bolder with Jayden. Funnier. Relaxed.

"Okay, here's the test, Your Highness—"

"Don't call me that," I warned. I gave him a playful shove.

Darkness descended.

"Your Royal Harvest? Queen of the Farm Where There Is No Farm?" Jayden strung together a stream of silly titles.

I caught sight of Spirit Boy from the corner of my eye. He'd appeared alongside us. Anger pulsed around him, sending out sparks.

Ignore him. Ignore him.

"What's my test?" Through the dimming light, I focused my attention on Jayden.

He placed the pudding cup in my right hand, then reached for Tamara's half-eaten cheese stick, which he placed into my left. "Dunk and down. That's the test."

"Go for it, Sara!" Lily cheered loudly. I had an audience.

"No problem." Cheddar cheese and chocolate were gross together, but it wasn't the worst possible combination.

As I lifted the cheese stick toward the cup, the large room grew even darker. A hum, faint at first, then louder, filled my ears. The noise drowned out the banging of trays.

Before I could react, the spirit rushed toward me with incredible speed. He bumped me hard with his shoulder.

My arm flew forward, and the dark-brown pudding rocketed out of the cup, landing with a loud splat across my cheek and in my hair. Thick globs slid down my face and onto my collar. The creamy substance lodged inside my ear. I wiped frantically at my hair, but that only made it worse.

Everyone laughed. The noise echoed in the packed room, bouncing off the walls and reverberating in my clogged ear. I felt my eyes fill with tears and I willed myself not to cry.

The entire cafeteria had witnessed me throw a cup

of pudding at myself. Now they were all laughing.

All except Jayden's bodyguard. Arms crossed and brow furrowed, he stared at me with angry eyes, letting me know that *he* was in charge.

CHAPTER 10

I left.

No explanation. No laughing at myself. No asking a teacher for a pass. I just stood and speed-walked to the girls' bathroom.

No one would understand what had happened. Ever.

The large bathroom was empty. The combined odor of bleach, urine, and fruity lip gloss clung to the peach-tiled walls. I shivered. The temperature felt twenty degrees colder in here than in the hall. I leaned both hands on the chipped white sink and stared at my pudding makeover in the scratched mirror.

Gross!

Of course there were no paper towels. Just those stupid hand dryers. Grabbing a roll of toilet paper, I mopped the chocolate from my face and scooped it from my ear. I stuck half my head under the sink faucet, desperate to return my sticky hair back to blond.

The noise took a moment to work its way into my brain.

Crying. Muffled sobs.

I hesitated, the icy water washing the pudding down the drain, and strained my ears.

Was someone here?

I shut off the faucet. Combing my fingers through my hair, I stood and listened. Water dripped onto my shoulder.

A faint sob. A choked sniffle.

I whirled around and scanned the bathroom. No feet peeked out from any of the four stalls. "Hello?" I called. "Who's here?"

No answer.

More sniffles.

Every nerve in my body tingled. High alert.

I wasn't alone. I could feel it. Bits of wet, disintegrating toilet paper dropped from my dripping hair to the floor, but I didn't move.

Another sniffle.

"I know you're here!" I had wanted to shout it, but my voice came out in a forced whisper.

And then she appeared.

A girl. She shimmered into view in the far corner. She wore a short-sleeved white blouse, a tan calf-length skirt, white ankle socks, and loafers. A pale-pink cardigan sweater hung over her shoulders, fastened by only the top button. Her figure vibrated as if she was standing under a strobe light.

My fingers wrapped around the porcelain sink for support.

I stared at her. She stared at me.

Water soaking through my shirt shook me out of my daze. *Get away*, I thought. *Just get away.*

With a gasping breath, I pried my fingers from the sink and forced my feet toward the door.

"No . . . please . . . don't go . . ." Low, grief-stricken sobs echoed off the tiles. "Please . . ."

I stopped. *Get away*, the voice screamed in my head.

"Please . . ."

"Why?" Was I an idiot? Why was I talking to this girl . . . this *spirit*?

"I need you. I need your help."

"Me? You don't need me."

"I'm Alice. We're the same age, you know." Her voice was soft.

"How do you know my age?" I still hadn't moved. Neither had she. A standoff in the girls' bathroom.

"I know all about you, Sara." She dabbed her eyes with a white cotton handkerchief. Her eyelashes were unusually long. "I've been waiting for someone like you. I've been waiting . . . so long."

Enough, the voice inside me cried. *Stop talking. Leave.*

"Waiting for what?" My mouth wasn't listening to the voice.

Alice moved slowly toward me. Chestnut hair in stiff waves, as if set in large curlers overnight, framed her narrow face. Pink lipstick stained her lips. She stopped several feet away. "I went to Stellamar Middle School too. Like you." Her voice was steady, more controlled now. "And like you, I was running for Harvest Queen. Of course, that was back in 1952—"

"1952?" I blurted. Suddenly pieces fit together. "Did you—were you the one who put that flyer thing in my locker? And the other stuff?"

Alice gave me a tight-lipped smile. "They were supposed to be hints."

"Hints for what?" I found myself closing the gap between us. "How was I supposed to know they were hints? From you?"

She raised her arm, as if to stop me. "I really wanted to be Harvest Queen. But look at me. I was too plain. I'm not beautiful like you."

She stopped in front of the mirror. I gazed into the glass. At the doors of the toilet stalls behind me. Alice had no reflection. As if she didn't exist.

"My parents both worked at the college. Professors. Higher learning was their dream. I got good grades and studied hard for them. But that's not what I wanted." She pulled a tube of lipstick from the pocket of her skirt. Removing the cap, she carefully applied the pink color to her already made-up mouth. "My parents hated makeup. They threw away the movie magazines I bought. They called them frivolous."

A fat tear formed in the corner of her eye. "It was all I dreamed of. Hollywood. Beauty pageants. The glamour." She pushed the tear away. "I had a plan, you know. A plan to change everything. I was going to be glamorous and beautiful when I grew up."

I didn't say anything. But I didn't leave, either. I listened to Alice's story.

"I signed up to run for Harvest Queen. I made posters. I gave kids little gifts to vote for me. I convinced them that I would be the perfect Harvest Queen." She raised her hands to her head, as if indicating a crown. "My parents didn't even know I was running. I planned to surprise them at the parade when my name was called. With that crown on my head, doors would open. I would enter beauty pageants. I would go to Hollywood, and my parents would understand that this was my true destiny."

"Then what happened?"

"Then it all got ruined." Alice sighed. "I woke one morning with a sore throat. Nothing horrible. I went to school. I had a test that day I didn't want to miss because I had studied so hard for it. I swear, I wasn't that sick, Sara! But I got worse so quickly. Soon I had a high fever and was having trouble breathing. The next day I was rushed to the hospital. I don't remember much of that day. I was burning with fever. Then it was over."

"Over?" I didn't understand.

"My dreams . . . my plans . . . my life was over. I died in that hospital. I died alone. My family couldn't come into the room to see me. I had a disease . . . a deadly, contagious disease. Polio." Tears streamed down her translucent cheeks.

"That's so horrible." I reached for the roll of toilet paper perched on the edge of the sink, but she shook her head. Her handkerchief materialized, and she wiped her eyes.

"It gets worse. The next day five more kids were brought to the hospital with polio. The day after, another seven. Many died. Others were paralyzed. The newspapers called it an epidemic." She sniffed, then swallowed hard. "The mayor canceled the Harvest Parade and Dance. There were to be no public gatherings. Everyone hid in their homes, petrified of catching polio. No girl was crowned that year."

"I'm sorry."

"But I'm still here. I'm still in middle school," Alice said. She leveled her gaze against mine. "I'm stuck here."

I gave her a questioning look. I was new to this. I didn't understand.

"I wanted to be Harvest Queen. It's my destiny," she said simply. "I *need* to be Harvest Queen."

"But how—?"

"You. You, Sara. Don't you see?" She moved forward until we were only inches apart. The icy air that had flowed from my locker now projected from her. "When you arrived, I could feel it. Your energy. Our connection. You're my answer. With you, I can finally wear that crown."

"But I don't want to be Harvest Queen!" How many times would I have to say this?

"It's not for you, Sara. It's for me. That's why I signed you up."

"I should have been given a choice—"

Someone coughed. A forced, fake cough.

I whirled around, toward the door. Lily stared wide-eyed at me.

How long had she been there?

"Hi," I said meekly. "I—uh—think I got all the pudding out. Right?" I tried to act natural.

Lily took a tentative step toward me. "Yeah, it's gone." She seemed unsure, which was so not like her. "I'm sorry we all laughed. It wasn't funny."

"It was, kind of." I pushed out a smile. Alice retreated to the corner but watched intently.

"Listen, you're obviously freaked out about the Harvest Queen thing. I"—her words spilled out in a rush—"I heard you talking to yourself. That's not good. I'll go to the principal with you. I'll help you get out of it."

"It's not your fault," I told her. I shot Alice a meaningful look. It was *her* fault. "Principal Bowman kind of scares me."

"Me too, right? With that laser stare . . ." Lily and I left the bathroom together.

I felt bad for Alice. I truly did.

But I wasn't going to risk my friendship with Lily to help a dead girl. Just because I could see and hear her didn't mean I had to do what she wanted.

CHAPTER 11

I sat cross-legged on the wide porch that wrapped around the front of our house. It was still brutally hot. I hoped Dad would take me to the beach when he got home.

Lady Azura sat in an oversize wicker chair and flipped through the copy of *People* I'd just gotten her at the corner store. She sniffed, then mumbled something about "fools." But that was all she said. Since Friday night, she hadn't tried to talk to me about spirits or powers or any of it. She acted as if our midnight snack hadn't even happened. She just had me get things at the store or dust the crystals that lined her glass shelves.

I arranged my binders and books in a semicircle around me. I'd start my homework on the left and work my way to the right. Blue math binder first. The Harvest Queen flyer from my locker fluttered to the floor as I opened it.

I traced the date with my finger.

Alice.

As hard as I tried, I couldn't stop thinking about her.

It was unfair, her getting sick and all. She had wanted to win so badly.

Not your problem, that little voice in my head countered.

I bit my lip, unsure.

"A battle is brewing within you. A conflict between your inner and outer self," Lady Azura commented.

I looked over at her. She held my gaze, then turned back to her magazine.

I examined the old flyer again. The thick paper. The faded ink. It spoke of a time long ago. A time I didn't know.

Then it hit me. Lady Azura would know! She'd always lived in Stellamar. She was even Harvest Queen herself. Would she remember Alice? I tried to do the math. Lady Azura was older than Alice would have been if she'd lived, but still . . .

I could ask her about Alice. We didn't have to speak about powers and connections with spirits and all that. I could pretend it was a school project. Some sort of research thing.

"Did you live here in 1952?" I held up the flyer.

Lady Azura placed the magazine in her lap. "Child, if you want me to see that, you better move yourself closer. I may be able to see into the future, but I can't see the present without my glasses. And they're inside."

I stood and handed her the flyer. She squinted at it. "Harvest Festival." She tilted her head. "Do you know I've only missed one in all my years? When my Diana was born. People said it was fitting that my daughter arrived on that very day. I called her my little queen. But I must say, they all blur together now."

This was the first time I'd heard about a daughter. I'd never thought about Lady Azura having a family. About her being a mother. She didn't talk about kids or a husband. I wondered where they were.

"What's so interesting about this particular festival?" she asked, jolting me out of my thoughts.

"It was the year it was canceled. Some disease called polio, I think."

"Of course." She nodded. "A terrible time. So many children fell ill. My neighbor's son spent the rest of his days in a wheelchair, his legs paralyzed by polio."

"There was a girl named Alice who died. Alice"—I realized I didn't know her last name—"something. I'm not sure, but she was around my age. She was running for Harvest Queen."

Lady Azura's usually bright eyes clouded over. She crossed her legs, then recrossed them. Her knobby knees poked up from beneath her long mauve skirt. "I know of Alice."

"You do?"

"Why are you asking about Alice, Sara?"

"There's this school project—"

"No, there isn't," she interrupted me calmly. Matter-of-fact.

Was I that bad a liar? Or could she sense when people didn't tell the truth? Suddenly it didn't matter. She wasn't Lily. I didn't have to pretend.

"Okay, it's not that. I can see Alice."

"Alice caused this town a lot of pain." Lady Azura

rubbed her thin hands together. She didn't seem concerned that I could see Alice.

"How?"

"Alice Emerson brought polio to Stellamar." Anger laced her voice. For a moment neither of us spoke, listening to the sound of young kids calling to one another down the street. They sounded like Lily's brothers.

"Really?" I recalled Alice's tearstained face. She didn't look like someone who would have wanted to make a bunch of kids sick.

"Alice was the first, people said. She went to school with symptoms. She infected the others. She was the spark that started the fire." Lady Azura adjusted her legs again.

"But maybe she didn't know that she was sick."

"Maybe," Lady Azura agreed. She paused to consider what I'd said, and it was clear she was pained by the memory of that time. After a few moments, she spoke again. "When children die, people are angry. They lash out. We pointed our fingers at Alice, although by then the poor girl's body was buried in the old cemetery behind your school. Alice's parents were forced to move. The family were outcasts."

"That's not fair," I protested.

Lady Azura stared off into the distance. "I suppose you are right. But all those parents were looking for an answer to explain their children's deaths. Right or wrong, they blamed Alice and got their answer."

Everyone hated Alice. Was she guilty of getting kids sick? If she was, I didn't want to talk to her again.

"What does Alice want?" Lady Azura asked.

"Want?"

"They always want something."

I told her about the locker presents from Alice, how she'd distracted the principal, and the conversation in the bathroom. "But I'm not doing it."

"She came to you, Sara. To you." Lady Azura leaned forward. "She needs you."

"So what?"

"You are special. You have abilities that others do not. You also have the ability to end unhappiness and suffering. To allow these tortured souls to move on. And that is the greater ability."

"Move on from what?"

"Alice is trapped, like so many spirits are. She is

stuck, endlessly wandering the halls of middle school. Victory as Harvest Queen may be the key to release." Lady Azura stood. "You can unlock her door."

"I can't, even if I wanted to," I protested.

"You need confidence." She pulled a shiny white cord out from under her billowy ivory blouse. Three long crystals hung from the cord. She removed a beautiful bluish-green-colored one. "This is aquamarine. The stone of courage." She pressed it into my palm. "You must first face your fears. Then you can do great things."

"But I still have that ruby crystal," I protested. I'd stopped bringing it to school. I'd even stopped sleeping with it. I feared it was backfiring, somehow causing that angry spirit to appear between me and Jayden. I'd buried it deep in my sock drawer. "I don't think this one will—"

"There is great courage within you, Sara. I can feel it. You are stronger than you know." Lady Azura opened the front door with no explanation of where she was going. "Keep both gemstones. Activate that courage. Then you will be able to do what is right."

I stared at the crystal in my hand long after she left.

"Can I help you?" Esther leaned on the main office counter, sorting field trip permission forms into piles.

"Principal Bowman wants to see me." I produced the note that had been sent to my social studies class.

Esther pointed to the door behind her without looking up from her sorting. "Go on."

I should've brought Lily, I thought, as I walked tentatively toward the office. But I didn't know what class she was in now or how I could get her out.

"Come, sit," Principal Bowman said, her attention on her computer screen. "I wanted to revisit our conversation." She scrolled down the page, her eyes moving from left to right. "I realized last night—I always realize these things at three in the morning—that you may not be aware of the assembly," she said, glancing up at me.

"The assembly?"

"There is a schoolwide assembly this week for the candidates to announce their proposed community service project."

"Community service project?" I couldn't stop parroting her.

"Harvest Queen is not a beauty contest. It's about being a model for your peers and giving back to the community. The winner will lead the school in the community service project that she campaigns with. That's what's important."

"I see." That made the whole queen thing less shallow, but it didn't change my mind. "I still don't—"

The temperature in the office dropped. The chill washed over me, causing me to shudder. The sudden cold forced me to lick my already chapped lips.

"Please . . . please . . . I need your help."

Alice. Standing alongside my chair. Reaching out for me.

"Esther, did you just turn on the air?" Principal Bowman shouted out the open door.

"I need this, Sara. They think . . ." She began to sob.

Esther yelled back. No air was turned on.

"I may have been the first one to get sick, but it wasn't my fault. I didn't ask to get sick." Tears glittered on Alice's shimmering face.

"Weird," Principal Bowman muttered. She began to button her thin sweater. "So, Sara, you've made up your mind?"

Alice rested her hand on my shoulder. I couldn't feel her actual touch. Instead I was overcome with sadness. Sadness so deep and so confusing, my body trembled. Everything around me slowed as her grief and yearning crawled deep inside me.

"Did you know that no one has ever laid flowers on my grave? I'm hated," she said between the tears. "I need to be more than the Girl Who Caused the Epidemic. I *need* to be Harvest Queen."

I blinked hard. Alice's tears were becoming my tears. I could feel her pain, her need to prove that she was more than the cause of others' misery.

My hand found the aquamarine tucked into my jeans pocket, and I spoke before I could think. I spoke for Alice.

"I changed my mind," I told Principal Bowman. "I'm going to run for Harvest Queen."

CHAPTER 12

Everyone was confused.

Especially Lily.

I don't blame her. I sounded crazy. I told her on our walk home that I was going through with it. I mean, she'd caught me yesterday alone in the bathroom yelling that I refused to be Harvest Queen. So I told her Principal Bowman convinced me to do it.

It wasn't a lie. She did.

Kind of.

Lily dropped her backpack on the curb and narrowed her eyes. "Are you doing this to be with the popular eighth-grade girls, or to prove some point that Avery's babbling about, or did you really get bullied into it?"

"I don't care about any other girls. I just moved

here, so I have no idea what Avery's deal is. This thing just started happening and wouldn't go away, and now I'm in it." I hoped she wouldn't be angry or disgusted with me. "Okay?"

"Okay. I don't really get it, but okay," she said, her mood changing right before my eyes. Her cheeks turned rosier, and her eyes widened. "If you're doing it, then let's really do it."

"What?"

Lily grabbed her backpack, pulled out her phone, and started furiously texting. "Campaign meeting at my house this afternoon. I'll invite Avery and Marlee. Maybe Tamara and Nisha, and maybe even Miranda." She smiled at me, her fingers still tapping. "If you're in it, let's win it!"

I smiled back at her. I was glad Lily was there to help me. I was glad that she didn't judge me like the girls in my old school.

I wished I could tell her about Alice.

I told Lady Azura.

"Now what do I do?" I asked, as she lit the many candles around her fortune-telling room.

The rare client was due soon.

"Do? When I won, I recall making a beautiful poster. And a speech. Yes, I wrote a speech. I can't recall about what." She produced a can of cinnamon room spray and began spritzing.

"Not that regular stuff. I mean, like, supernatural or with that other sense you said I have. How do I use that to win? To help Alice?"

"You don't."

"What? But I thought—I mean, I thought I could do something, or you could show me how . . ." The fluttering in my stomach started again. I never thought she wouldn't help. She was the one who'd told me to do this.

She produced a cloth and rubbed the crystal ball. "Sara, I don't have a magic wand. I don't have the ability to fix elections or change the way people think. Maybe you do, but I doubt it."

"What do I do about Alice?" My voice had gotten squeaky again. "How do I win Harvest Queen?"

"You are already helping Alice. Remember, you made a choice, not her. It may be her desire, but it is your will. As for winning—" The front doorbell chimed.

"Mrs. McHugh is here." Lady Azura headed toward the foyer. She rested her hand on the doorknob. "As for winning, I personally like a catchy slogan." She opened the door, letting Mrs. McHugh in and me out. "I know! Maybe something that rhymes with Sara?"

Mascara? Sahara? French Riviera? Christina Aguilera? Nothing good rhymes with Sara, I realized as I walked down to Lily's house.

I didn't have a slogan. I didn't have a community service idea, even though Avery had already texted me a list of lame possibilities. And I certainly didn't have a speech. How was I ever going to get up in front of everyone and give a speech? Suddenly I hated Alice.

"A postcard from my aunt. She's in San Antonio." Mrs. Randazzo stood by their mailbox at the end of their circular driveway. She held up a postcard of an armadillo in a cowboy hat.

"Funny picture." I really liked Lily's mom. She looked like Lily, except grown up. I liked how she talked to me like I was her niece or even her daughter. At mealtimes, she just set another place for me. No questions asked.

"Aunt Lorena always had a wacky sense of humor. Not like Aunt Fran. Now that was a bitter woman."

I didn't get it at first. Maybe because Lily had more relatives than our town had people. Then I remembered Fran. Fran who made the banana bread. I pushed the toe of my sneaker into the white pebbles covering their driveway. "Really?" I said softly.

"But she did know about the tomatoes, I hear." Mrs. Randazzo gathered her mail, and turned to me and smiled. "I made the chocolate cake today. With tomatoes."

"I didn't mean for—"

"You'll try it inside. Very moist." She placed a hand on my arm and gave the smallest squeeze. "Exactly like my mother's."

I didn't know what to say. Did she suspect? "A lucky guess," I mumbled.

"Luck is a beautiful thing. Lady Azura has a way with luck. She once told my fortune years ago. I thought it was silly at the time. Then, recently, when certain things happened that I believed were luck, I remembered what she said, and I wonder if it wasn't fate."

"She told my fortune too," I confessed. "She said I'd meet this cute boy at school."

"Did you?"

"I did. But it's not working out right."

"Why not?" Mrs. Randazzo had a way of listening as if every word you said mattered to her.

"I thought he liked me back. It seemed that way, but then . . ." I'd gotten this far and didn't know where to go. How to explain the spirit? "It's like he gets pushed away."

"Maybe he is intimidated by you, Sara. People often put up walls between themselves and what scares them," Mrs. Randazzo explained, as we walked up to and into the house. "Give it time. Emotional walls do crumble."

There was no chance Spirit Boy was crumbling. His wall was built of iron, steel, and whatever force he had to keep me and Jayden far from each other.

"What are you guys talking about?" Lily called. She, Tamara, Avery, and Marlee were already gathered around markers and paper on her kitchen table. Lily's aunt Angela was there too, watching Lily's four-year-old sister and her two kids coloring on the floor in a corner. Miranda hadn't shown, but that didn't surprise me. Helping me probably wasn't high on her list of fun things to do.

"Talking about boys," Mrs. Randazzo said in a singsong voice.

A flurry of excited chatter about the boys and the upcoming dance followed. No one was going with a date. That would be too weird. But they were hoping that the boys would actually get on the dance floor. And dance. With them.

"Luke likes Sara," Tamara announced.

"I think Sara likes Jayden Mendes," Lily said knowingly.

"I used to, but not anymore," I replied softly. What was the point? I was scared what Spirit Boy would do to me if I went near Jayden at the dance.

"Mendes?" Aunt Angela asked. I wasn't sure if she was Lily's mom's sister, or her dad's, or if she was related at all. Sometimes Lily called her parents' close friends aunt and uncle too. "The Mendes family lives on our street."

"What are they like?" Lily asked, always curious.

"They moved in last year. Just the one boy, as far

as I can tell. They seem nice enough, except there's something, well, off, about them."

"Off?" Lily's mom asked, concerned.

"They just seem sad. The parents. It's weird, right?" Angela twirled her long, dark hair. "They never said anything about it. But it's like they carry it with them."

We asked Angela more questions, but she didn't know why they seemed so sad to her. They just did. "I feel like so many people have secrets," she said. She was talking to Lily's mom, but I was listening. "There must be secrets in every house, in every building, everywhere in this town. It's a shame people are afraid to ask questions."

"One more poster done!" Avery announced. She held up a sign with my name.

"Great," I said. "And I just came up with a community service project."

It was time to tell some secrets.

I stood trembling in the wings of the school stage a few days later.

What was I doing here? I wondered.

I felt as if I'd suddenly woken from a long sleep. A

long, delusional sleep. I'd been so involved in taking photos for the project I'd cooked up, and my new friends had rallied around me, spending our afternoons together making posters and having fun, that I'd lost track of what this really was.

Me. Alone on a stage. Running for Harvest Queen.

For Alice.

Alice, who I hadn't seen since that day in the principal's office.

This was such a bad idea. *Bad, bad, bad.*

I twisted the silver braided ring I always wore and stared out onto the enormous stage. *I can't go out there. I can't.*

My fingers frantically searched the cotton folds of my navy-and-white skirt. Pocket? Where was the pocket?

I had no pocket.

The realization hit like a punch in the stomach. The aquamarine lay in the pocket of my jeans, now crumpled on my bedroom floor.

The stone of courage was on my bedroom floor.

And I was here.

Where was I going to find courage?

The pounding started behind my eyes. Pulsing. In time with my racing heart. *I have to leave,* I thought.

I turned, and she was there.

Alice.

No longer crying. Happy.

"It's our turn soon."

"No," I whispered. My eyes darted frantically across the backstage area. Lots of girls milled about. No one very near. Avery had gone to find me a hairbrush. She'd be back soon. I couldn't be seen talking to the air. And that was all they would ever see. Not Alice. Air.

"I can't," I whispered. "I'm sorry." I started to walk away. To leave. Quit.

Alice stopped me with her icy touch. "I *need* you. We can do this."

And again, her desire coursed through me. I stood a prisoner in her frigid cage.

"Watch," she commanded. And I stayed and looked as Dina finished her speech and Chloe stepped onto the stage. The lights were trained on her. Everyone watched as she began to speak about littering and cleaning school grounds.

Chloe was athletically built but short, and from

where I stood, I could see her lifting up on her toes behind the podium to reach the microphone. She droned on about garbage, then sneezed. A short, fast, high-pitched sneeze. Then another.

Startled, she fumbled, then remembered where she'd left off. Calf muscles straining, she pulled herself up to her full height, rallying for respect of school property.

Another sneeze—this one huge—racked her body. Three more followed. Each time she managed a sentence, her body convulsed with the force of a sneeze.

The giggles started softly, but soon the audience couldn't hold back their delight. Chloe was like some strange windup sneezing doll. Each sneeze was wetter and wilder, until she could no longer speak. Chloe fled, sneezing, from the stage.

I stole a glance at Alice. She was watching the stage.

Christine was next, but she could not find the copy of her speech. Principal Bowman changed the order and hurried Ava Gomez into the bright light.

Ava looked as nervous as I felt. She grasped the podium as she began to speak. Something about inviting senior citizens to take classes with us. I cringed. Having Lady Azura at school, telling the fortunes of all my friends, would be more than I could handle. Ava droned on. Boring.

Alice kept her eyes focused on the stage. She wouldn't look at me. Icy air swirled about us.

Christine still couldn't find her speech. Or the second copy she had tucked into her locker. She refused to go on.

Caroline sauntered confidently onto the stage. The audience broke into applause. Avery, who was now by my side, whispered, "Everyone loves her. She's like a goddess in this school."

As if I needed to be freaked out even more.

Caroline waved and smiled. Everyone cheered. But that was all she did. Smile. Wave. Giggle. Smile.

After a few minutes, Principal Bowman hurried onto the stage. She pulled Caroline aside and whispered intently. Caroline shrugged and gave her brightest goddess smile. Principal Bowman scowled, the only one not blinded by Caroline's beauty.

Then Principal Bowman nudged Caroline off the stage. Caroline, for the first time, stopped smiling. Her perfect peachy-pink skin turned blotchy with outrage. The principal announced into the microphone that Caroline's inability to come prepared with a community service project had caused her instant disqualification.

Caroline looked completely confused. So did all the kids. Everyone had assumed Caroline would be Harvest Queen. The assembly was just a formality to get out of class. Caroline tried to explain that she could come up with something. She just needed a minute or two.

It didn't matter.

"The mayor is talking to Principal Bowman." Avery pointed to the other side of the stage. "He's angry. He takes this mega-seriously."

But I was looking at Alice. The temperature dropped as her smile grew.

Could Alice somehow be doing this? I wondered.

"Our final candidate today is Sara Collins," Principal Bowman announced.

Hands clapped as I stared, mouth open, at Alice.

"It's your turn," she said, and pushed me onto the stage.

CHAPTER 13

I stumbled toward the podium.

Avery hurried out behind me, a laptop tucked under her arm. I stood awkwardly as she connected the laptop to the auditorium's multimedia system. I felt bad that I'd suspected her of doing something selfish. Avery had masterminded this whole campaign. I owed her. Big-time.

I just hoped she wouldn't be too disappointed when I lost.

Alice. Avery. They were both counting on me.

My legs wouldn't stop shaking behind the podium. I tried not to sway, as I clicked on my PowerPoint presentation. Another one of Avery's ideas. She knew public speaking was not my thing. But I was great at taking photos and manipulating them on my computer.

"My community service idea is a living history project." My voice sounded abnormally loud through the microphone. Oh God, was that Jayden to the far right?

Don't look at the faces in the front rows, I commanded myself. *Pretend they're not here.*

The melody of Lady Azura's chickadee song popped into my head. The chorus repeating, over and over.

Courage. Have courage.

I focused on the photo montage I'd created, playing on the enormous screen. Pop music synced to the images thumped behind it.

The town hall. The haunted house on the boardwalk. The school. The large bank clock that never told the right time. The broken-down pier. The lighthouse.

Pictures I had taken around Stellamar.

I explained that even though I had just moved here, I could tell right off that Stellamar had a rich history. I had gone to the small local library, but there was very little about the town and its people.

More photos layered like a collage: Lady Azura years ago as Harvest Queen. Lily's uncle, who owned the pizza place. Lily's cousin Dawn Marie in her hideous pink dress as Harvest Queen.

"Our school would create a living history through interviews, photos, and videos to trace the stories of those still living in Stellamar and those who have died," I said.

Even more photos: George Marasco, who'd built the boardwalk years ago. Alice's gravestone in the small graveyard behind our school. The newspaper headline from 1952 about polio that Avery had uncovered online.

"History shouldn't be a secret. For example, did you know that the guy who built Stellamar's boardwalk, George Marasco, used to let poor kids during the Depression ride the rides for free? And did you know that the Harvest Festival was canceled one year because one of the girls running for queen brought polio into the school? This project will let future generations know the truth—good and bad—about our town."

People clapped. Not a lot. Mostly teachers, I suspected.

I did it, I thought as I hurried off. *I stood on that stage and spoke.* I'd never done anything like that before. It might not have been great, but I did my best.

Avery jumped up and down and hugged me. I could hear Lily's squeal as she ran toward me.

Then I saw Alice. No longer smiling. Cold air swirling about her.

Clearly she didn't think my best was good enough.

Christine wasn't in science.

Normally I wouldn't notice, but today was Friday. Voting day. The Harvest Festival was tomorrow. The dance tomorrow night. How could she not be here?

Plus, she was my new lab partner.

I calculated the life cycle of a star by myself.

Jayden sat across the classroom, now paired with Marlee. They worked quietly. No joking.

I was kind of glad.

He looked up, and our eyes connected. He must have felt me staring.

Then, out of nowhere, Jayden's worksheet fluttered and blew off the table. He turned away. Bent down to retrieve it.

No open windows. No air-conditioning vents.

But I'd seen what happened.

The angry spirit messing with things.

Keeping me away.

Christine appeared just as class was ending.

"Where were you?" I asked. "The lab was impossible. I don't know if my answers are right."

"Whatever. It doesn't matter." Her voice fell flat. Her shoulders slumped.

"What's wrong?" I asked, as we filed into the hall.

"They kicked me out of the running. I can't run for Harvest Queen! Principal Bowman said it was only fair to disqualify me, since Caroline got disqualified for not having given a speech."

"Christine, I'm so sorry." I felt horrible. "I really am. I know how much you wanted it. That just seems so unfair."

"Whatever. I guess I'll vote for you now." She stopped at a locker and opened the door, our conversation over.

"Sara! Sara!" Avery called from down the hall.

I pushed through a crush of bodies to catch up with her.

"Why aren't you smiling?" she demanded.

Where to begin?

"You need to smile today," she instructed. "People vote for happy people. You should say hi and talk, too."

"I think I'll stick with the smiling," I said. "I'm better at it." I forced a smile at a passing girl.

"Fine. It won't matter much anyway." Avery's lips curled in as if trying to hold back a secret that was desperate to escape.

"Why?" I asked suspiciously. Avery had come up with crazy schemes all week. Each one I'd refused to let her go through with.

"You'll see! It's genius!" she called, and darted into her art classroom before I could get it out of her.

The ballots were passed out during last period.

Dina. Ava. Chloe. Sara.

I stared at my name.

Sara Collins.

Could I really vote for myself?

My pen doodled along the margin of the paper. Flowers. Vines connecting them. Then I felt my hand lift.

Higher.

I watched as if it were no longer attached to my body. The pen moved toward the names. Toward my name.

A hand rested on mine.

Guiding me.

I turned slightly as my pen circled *Sara Collins*.

Alice.

I was certain I'd failed her. One of the eighth graders would win. Everyone knew them and liked them.

Would Alice be trapped in this school forever? I wondered. Was there another way to help her?

The teacher collected the ballots.

And Alice still held my hand.

CHAPTER 14

I grabbed my dad's hand, caught up in the excitement, as the high school marching band high-stepped and drum-rolled their way down the boardwalk. Girls with frosted eye shadow and blue-fringed leotards threw batons and twirled enormous flags in time with the syncopated calls of the trumpets and trombones.

Trucks, vans, and even bicycles rolled past, each decorated with miles of colorful crepe paper and balloons. The coast guard, in their starched white uniforms, threw bags of Swedish fish to the children who lined the route.

The entire town had turned out Saturday morning for the parade, which ran the entire length of the boardwalk and onto Beach Drive. Lily watched with her brothers and sister down the way. I recognized kids and teachers from school throughout the crowd. The summer smells of fudge and cotton candy had been replaced with spicy apple cider and the first pumpkin bread of the season. Even the weather had begun to change. Cooler air blew in off the ocean, breaking down the humidity.

"You should be sitting on a float," my dad said to Lady Azura.

"I should, shouldn't I?" Lady Azura stood beside me and beamed. Today was one of the few times she ventured out into the world, and she'd certainly dressed for it, in a long red dress with flowing kimono-like sleeves. Her metallic "walking-around" sneakers matched the oversize gold sun hat on her head.

"A royal float. They should have a float for former queens to honor those of us who refuse to let go of our glamour." Lady Azura scanned the crowd. "Sadly, there'd be very few riders. Unlike me, most of these women traded their glamour in for a life of pizza and fried clams."

This made my dad laugh.

I stood between them, watching uneasily. Since we'd moved in, I'd had trouble deciding whether they liked each other. Sometimes they spoke as if they were long-lost friends and other times as if they'd just been introduced at an awkward back-to-school night.

"Is she here?" Lady Azura whispered to me.

"No. I don't think she can leave the school."

"They should be announcing the winner soon."

"I've been thinking." I stole a glance at my dad. He was completely absorbed by the fire truck, piled high with vegetables and other harvest-type stuff, coming down the route. "What if I tried to get Alice—or her spirit—to Hollywood or a beauty pageant instead? Get her a different crown somehow—"

"You are too focused on the crown." Lady Azura spoke in a low voice. "The crown may just be a symbol of something that Alice desires. Like a child who holds a blanket wants security."

"But she asked me for the *crown*. And I tried. I really did, but I can't give her that. She didn't ask me for security or . . ." I stopped talking and watched a familiar bald man in a dark suit climb onto a makeshift stage. Then I continued my thought. "What good is trying to help when you can't?"

The microphone screeched, then crackled with

static. All attention turned to the plywood stage.

"Welcome to the ninety-sixth annual Harvest Festival!" the bald man called. A huge cheer erupted. The band launched into the first bars of the school's fight song.

The bald guy turned out to be Stellamar's mayor. I'd seen him at the school assembly. He spoke about the town until little kids got bored and pelted one another with Swedish fish, then he boomed, "And now for the crowning of this year's middle-school Harvest Queen!"

In an instant, Lily and Avery found their way to me. They gathered close, buzzing with excitement.

"We have our fingers crossed for you," Avery said. "Toes, too."

My dad looked perplexed.

"This year's winner, chosen by both the students and teachers, is—" The mayor made a big deal about opening an envelope.

I felt bad. I should've told my dad, I realized. It shouldn't have been a secret.

The mayor pulled out a card.

Lily squeezed my hand.

I glanced over at Dad. Maybe Lady Azura was right.

Maybe I should tell him more things.

"Sara Collins!"

I watched Dad's eyebrows shoot upward.

"Sara! Sara!" Lily shouted my name.

"Sara! You won!" Avery pulled my arm, dragging me forward. Out onto the boardwalk.

I glanced back at my dad. He had his fists in the air. Huge grin on his face. Cheering for me.

Avery pulled me along. Up onto the stage. Next to the bald guy.

What was I doing up here? This couldn't be right.

The mayor placed a crown on my head. It slipped a bit to the side, and Avery reached up and straightened it. He handed me a large bouquet wrapped in crinkly cellophane. Pink carnations.

Everyone clapped. Faces everywhere. All looking at me!

"Quiet, please," the mayor said into the microphone. "I wanted to quickly talk about Sara's inspiring community service idea, which the middle school will begin tackling next month. It will celebrate and bring to life our town's history using the written word, recordings, photographs, and videos."

He pulled the microphone from the stand and held it in his hand. "I watched Sara's presentation, and I must say it moved me. She talked about unearthing the secrets of the past." He paused. "There was a photo she showed during her presentation of the gravestone of a girl named Alice Emerson." He paced across the stage. "Our town blamed Alice for bringing polio to the school. Many of you here may remember Alice, and the tragedy that happened in the fall of 1952."

A murmur arose, but the mayor continued to speak. "Alice lived down the street from my family before I was born. While growing up, I remember my parents talking about Alice. How they felt she was unfairly blamed for causing the polio outbreak. How she was one of *many* kids who'd attended a pool party a few weeks before in the town of Hadley, forty minutes away from here."

"I was at that pool party!" a white-haired man yelled from the side of the stage.

"Hadley's polio outbreak started before ours," the mayor continued. "The virus was there first."

"That's true, but we didn't realize it then. We were all too concerned with all the sick kids here in

Stellamar," the white-haired man replied.

"Alice was in the wrong place at the wrong time. A victim like the rest of the children." The mayor wiped a line of sweat beading his brow. "There is no one person to blame for the polio outbreak." He continued to pace. The entire town was quiet, hanging on his every word.

"Our town did something very wrong in our pain. We lashed out at one of our own. Generations of Stellamar residents singled out one girl. In that time of tragedy, we shouldn't have been pointing fingers. We should have been reaching out to hold hands. My parents and others like them—and this includes me, since I grew up hearing about this—never spoke up to clear her name. Not until now."

"I remember Alice," declared an older woman in a loud, clear voice. "She was very smart. And I recall that she loved the movies."

"It was a confusing time," the white-haired man added, sounding sad. "Poor Alice was just a victim."

"I want this town to be a place of understanding and open-mindedness. No whispering behind closed doors. No more hiding behind half-truths." The mayor reached his free hand toward the audience. "I invite you all to share your stories and your secrets with the middle schoolers of Stellamar and help us compile an honest record of the history of our town."

More applause.

Alice, I thought. *No one blames you anymore.*

I was stunned. I had done something. Something important, something that made a change.

Avery guided me off the stage. Kids surrounded me, but I couldn't focus. I wanted to get to the school. I needed to tell Alice.

Or did she already know somehow?

"Oh my God, it worked. It really worked," Avery was saying to Lily.

"What worked?" I asked, tuning in.

Avery grinned. "I told you it was genius."

"What did you do? How did you make me win?"

"It wasn't only me." Avery smiled slyly. "I got Jayden to help."

"Jayden?" I scanned the crowd. Was he here? I couldn't see him.

"We plotted it together." Avery couldn't contain her triumph. "You see, once Christine was kicked out, it left you as the only seventh grader against three eighth graders. I talked to all the seventh-grade girls and convinced them to vote for you. You know, to stick it to the eighth graders. And Jayden rallied the seventh-grade boys—they all think he's cool—and the seventh-grade girls who wouldn't listen to me but would definitely listen to a cute boy." Avery smiled proudly.

"I'm not understanding," I confessed.

"Do the math," Avery explained patiently. "Dina, Ava, and Chloe split the eighth-grade vote, but you got most of the seventh-grade vote. And the teachers. The teachers loved your speech. Loved that you actually gave it, at least."

"You won!" Lily cried. She pulled a pink carnation from my bouquet and tucked it behind her ear.

"I told you it would be awesome to have one of us wear the crown," Avery said.

One of us.

I was part of their group.

"Are you wearing your new dress tonight?" Miranda, who had appeared from the crowd, asked Lily. They were onto the dance already.

I searched the crowd flooding the boardwalk.

Brown hair everywhere. None belonging to Jayden. I wished I could find him.

He helped me win. But why?

He definitely thought the whole Harvest Queen thing was stupid. So did it mean he . . . liked me?

Suddenly I couldn't wait for tonight. Jayden was sure to be at the dance.

I wanted to talk to him. Alone.

CHAPTER 15

Lady Azura waited for me at the bottom of the stairs. "Where's the rest?"

"The rest of what?"

"The outfit." She squinted at my green dress with its flowy skirt and spaghetti straps. Aunt Charlotte had bought it for me before we left.

"Didn't anyone teach you about accessories?" Lady Azura sounded horrified. "I'll get you some jewelry. My rhinestones, perhaps?"

"No, no, I'm good. Really." I waved her off. I barely ever wore fancy dresses. Rhinestones were definitely out. "Besides, I have this." I held up the crown. "It's an accessory, right?"

She grinned. "The best kind."

I opened my other hand. "You can have this back."

Lady Azura gazed at the aquamarine. "Did it help?"

"I didn't use it," I admitted. "It was buried in my dirty clothes pile all this time." I paused. "I still have the ruby crystal, too. The love one." I held up the black wristlet bag that held my phone. "It's in here. I kind of want to keep it, if that's okay. For tonight."

"Keep them both. For tonight and for next time." She smiled knowingly and closed my fingers around the aquamarine. "There's always a next time. But wait here. . . . I still think you are under-accessorized!"

Rather than protest, I decided to wait and see what she would come back with. I could just put on whatever gaudy rhinestone thing she loaned me and then take it off as soon as I left the house.

But when Lady Azura returned a moment later, she wasn't holding a piece of gaudy rhinestone jewelry. She was holding a simple black cord with a silver clasp on the ends. She handed the cord to me. "You can place your crystal on the cord," she explained. I think the ruby crystal will look lovely around your neck tonight."

I looped the crystal onto the cord and fastened it around my neck. "How does it look?" I asked.

"Lovely. You are beautiful, Sara." Lady Azura beamed at me and squeezed my hand.

I noticed my dad standing there just then, watching us with a strange look on his face. He was holding his camera and started fiddling with it when he saw me looking at him.

"You do look lovely, Sara," he said. "Now smile and let me take a picture of my beautiful Harvest Queen!"

Dad snapped a few pictures, and I smiled obligingly. I usually hate having my picture taken, but tonight I was happy to pose for a couple of shots. I felt really good.

"I like that you're happy," Dad said as he snapped away.

I liked it too. I put on the crown so he could take a picture of me with it on.

Lily made me wear the crown as we walked into the school gym. I tried to protest, but she threatened to Krazy Glue it on my head. She said it was part of being Harvest Queen.

"If you don't wear it, I will," Avery offered.

"Back off. Sara let you ride on the float. She's

wearing the crown," Lily declared. And I did. Even though I felt ridiculous.

We walked through a balloon arch into the overheated gym. Kids clustered in groups around the dance floor.

The deep bass of the DJ's music thumped off the cinder-block walls. We passed a group of eighth-grade girls encased in a cloud of hairspray and perfume. I recognized Dina. She gave me the evil eye, then poked her friend, who glanced at the crown askew on my head and sneered.

"Jealous," Lily whispered.

I worried that I might have just made enemies as well as friends in this new school.

I trailed Lily and Avery to the drinks table, where the girls from our lunch table debated the fashion failures of the night.

I searched for Jayden.

To say thank you. To just see him . . . ? I didn't know.

"You didn't want to be queen, yet I say if the crown fits, wear it." Laughter echoed around me.

The gym teacher, still in his tracksuit, whistle

around his neck, appeared in front of me. "Still no sense of humor?"

I refused to answer. I wasn't even going to look at him.

"I will get you to laugh. Oh yes, I will. The school year has just begun." He pointed at me, then disappeared. His laughter trailed behind him.

I cringed. He was going to be a problem. A big one, I feared.

"I need to get some fresh air," I shouted to Lily above the roar of the music. I pointed to the open door at the back of the gym. She nodded, and I weaved my way through kids who were half dancing, half talking.

The gray sky held tight to the last rays of daylight. I sat on the second concrete step. She was here. I'd felt her when I first arrived.

"The crown. It's beautiful," Alice said. She materialized next to me. No longer weeping. Smiling. "I wanted the crown."

"I know." I told her about the mayor's speech and how her history would be rewritten.

"That pool party," she murmured. "I always believed it wasn't my fault. I just knew."

"Now everyone in town knows too." I touched the crown, still perched on my head. "This is yours. I did this for you. Or *you* did it—I'm not really sure."

"Thank you . . . it's ours . . . together." Her body glimmered in the pale light. "Let me help you now. Anything you need, just ask."

I stared at her shimmery body, fading in and out of focus. What could a dead girl do for me?

And then, a thought that I always carried with me in the far corner of my mind . . . Could I ask?

I played with the idea. Maybe she could. It was possible . . .

"Do you . . ." I hesitated. I didn't know what happened after death.

"Do I what?" Alice asked.

"Know my mother? Her name is Natalie Collins. She's dead." The words tumbled out. "Have you met her?"

"No." Alice shook her head. "There are lots of dead people. It's like asking if I know a boy named John who lives somewhere in the United States." She must have seen the hurt in my eyes. "I'm sorry."

I shrugged. I'd been hoping for years now to see

my mom. Instead I saw dead gym teachers.

"But I can help you find someone else. Someone living."

"Who?"

"Jayden. Oh, come on! Even I can see you like him. You do realize I watch you all the time at school." She smiled. "He's back there." She pointed past the lit soccer field to the small graveyard tucked beneath large maple trees.

"In the graveyard? *Your* graveyard?" I had gone in there last week to take the photo of her small tombstone.

"His father dropped him at the dance, but Jayden snuck around to the back of the school. He's been in the graveyard ever since."

"Is he alone?"

"Alone?" Alice asked.

"I mean, is there someone like you with him? A boy. Someone . . . not alive?" I wasn't sure how else to put it.

"I wouldn't know," Alice said. "You're the one who can see us. We can't all see each other. Strange, isn't it?"

"Very." I had to remember to ask Lady Azura if she knew about this.

"Find him," Alice urged. "I'm done here. I'm going."

"Going?"

"I don't know where. I hope Hollywood or someplace like it. I don't know how it all works, but I'm finally finished with middle school. I can move on now." Alice reached out to touch my crown.

Our crown.

A chill descended on me, but I fought the urge to shiver. I watched her smile one last time and then fade into the shadows. Gone.

I peered behind me into the crowded gym. Miranda stood a head taller than most of the other girls, and I easily spotted her by the table. She caught my eye and nudged Lily alongside her. Lily waved. I waved back.

I'll go fast, I thought. *No one will ever know.* Miss Klingert, who was monitoring the exit, had turned to cheer on the limbo showdown on the dance floor.

I hurried across the soccer field and through the wooden gate with the broken latch. Lights lining the field illuminated the crooked headstones. There were only about thirty, most tucked beneath the protective branches of three enormous maple trees.

ALICE ELIZABETH EMERSON

AUGUST 6, 1939—SEPTEMBER 23, 1952

I knelt in front of Alice's lonely grave. I lifted the crown off my head and gently placed it on top of the simple stone marker.

"This is yours," I said. "Now everyone will know who you really are. Harvest Queen."

"You're giving it away?"

He was here. I followed Jayden's voice to a nearby tree.

"I never really wanted it," I confessed. "It's not me."

"I didn't think so." He sat on the damp ground. The first leaves had begun to fall, decorating the dirt. Next to him stood a white stone marker, bigger and fancier than Alice's. "Why are you here?" he asked.

I glanced back at the crown perched regally on Alice's resting place. Or what I hoped would now be her resting place. "It's complicated. Who's that?" I nodded toward the headstone.

"I have no idea. It says his name is Thomas Ciccone."

"Why are you here, sitting in a graveyard, if you don't know this guy?"

"It felt weird to go to a party when I could look out the door and see a cemetery. I just couldn't do it tonight." He pushed a red leaf into the earth with his finger.

I didn't say anything.

"My brother died seven years ago. He is buried in a cemetery in Atlanta." Jayden kept his eyes on the leaf. "Marco was sixteen."

"I'm sorry." I knelt next to him.

"It felt more right to come up here. Even though I know he's obviously not here. You must think I'm weird."

"Not really. You miss your brother."

"Yeah. My mom and dad talk about Marco all the time. They are so sad. . . ." Jayden's voice trailed off as he became lost in his own thoughts.

And then it occurred to me: the spirit always by Jayden's side. The teenage boy in the hoodie. Was that Marco?

"He was a good guy. A great big brother." Jayden rested his hands on his thighs. "I never told anyone here about him."

"I won't tell," I promised.

Jayden slowly reached his hand toward mine.

Marco was there before I could react. I fell back into the dirt. I tumbled away from Jayden's touch.

"Are you okay?" Jayden asked, startled. I seemed to fall—or get pushed over—a lot around him.

"Fine," I said, wiping leaves from my skirt and scrambling to my feet.

I stared at Jayden. Stared at his brother. Did I dare say anything? Did I dare tell Jayden that his brother was standing between us?

"Sara? Sara? Is that you?" Lily and Miranda hurried across the soccer field. "Quick! The teachers are on patrol. What are you—" They spotted Jayden.

"Oh, well, hey." Lily smiled broadly at the two of us. "You should, uh, both get back."

"Thanks." Jayden seemed embarrassed. He headed abruptly toward the music, as if pushed forward by Marco.

"What were you guys doing?" Miranda demanded.

Lily grabbed my arm. "We need details," she whispered.

I walked with Lily and Miranda a few feet behind Jayden and the glimmering figure of Marco.

Jayden had tried to hold my hand. He *did* like me.

Marco ruined everything.

I wished I knew why he hated me.

Why was Marco even here? I wondered. Alice had been stuck in Stellamar for a reason. What kept Marco by Jayden's side? Had he been there for seven years?

I knew absolutely nothing about boys, but I wanted to get to know Jayden better. Without *him* messing it up.

But how?

I thought back to Lady Azura and our midnight talk. She said I had potential to do other things. What other things?

Did I have the power to make Jayden's brother go away?

There was a lot I needed to learn.

Want to know what happens to Sara next?

Here's a sneak peek at the next book in the series:

MISCHIEF NIGHT

Everything changes so fast.

Yesterday the rides and game stands were all open. The thump of repeating bass lines from the concert on the pier could be heard as far away as the lighthouse. Thousands of people milled about. Laughing. Shouting.

Today the boardwalk stood eerily quiet.

No music. No giggling toddlers. No guys haggling you to throw a softball at a milk bottle. Only a few screaming seagulls broke through the Sunday afternoon silence.

Summer in Stellamar was now officially over. Not officially in the calendar sense. That happened last month. Over, according to the boardwalk—and here in Stellamar, the boardwalk is everything. Last night was the annual October Boardwalk Bash, a town-wide good-bye party to the tourists, the lazy days in the sun, the ever-present carnival.

I lingered inside the doorway of the arcade and peered out at the now-shuttered stands and frozen Ferris wheel. Only the arcade, the pizza place, the ice cream place, and a hot dog stand or two braved the change of season. Heavy steel-colored clouds crept down to meet the dark waters of the Atlantic. The sand below the boardwalk's graying wood looked bleak, the colorful kaleidoscope of towels and umbrellas already a memory. The humidity had lifted, blown away along with the scents of cotton candy, popcorn, and grilled sausage and peppers.

Change was in the air.

Not a big deal for me. For the past three months, change was all I'd done. New town. New house. New school. New friends.

Lots of new.

Without the boardwalk, what would this New Jersey town be like? I wondered. I pulled my hands up into my sweatshirt sleeves. When summer came around again, would I be one of the group? A local? Would that ever happen? Or would I still be the quiet blond girl from California?

"Hey, Sara. Come play this!" Lily Randazzo called from inside the arcade.

My new friend.

Some new was good, I decided as I walked into the warm, yellow glow of the arcade. Lily's smile rivaled the bright video game lights. Maybe I can really fit in here, I thought. Lily waited by the skee-ball lanes with Miranda Rich and Avery Apolito.

"Let's see who can get the highest score," Miranda challenged us. Miranda liked to turn everything into a competition.

"I want to take home that pink bear." Avery pointed to an enormous fuzzy animal that resembled a fat dog more than a bear. Avery was one of the shortest girls in the seventh grade. The bear-dog, dangling on a hook from the wood-beamed ceiling, looked larger than her.

"There's no way." Lily twirled a strand of her long, dark hair around her finger, contemplating the prize. "It's too many tickets. You'd have to get every ball in the fifty slot for three games in a row. Try for that stuffed baseball with a face. It's only fifty tickets."

Avery scrunched her freckle-covered nose. "I have five of those already. My dog won't even play with them." She glanced around the arcade. There were maybe ten of us in the whole place. All summer it had been packed, but now it was just us. "Come on, Lily. Can't you do something?" Avery asked.

"Not here, Ave. Mr. Chopra isn't family." Lily lowered her voice. "In fact, I think he secretly hates my family. Thinks there's too many of us."

"There are a lot of you," Miranda quipped.

"The more the merrier, my mom says," Lily shot back with a grin.

"Two's company, three's a crowd, my mom says," Miranda countered.

"But four's a party—and so is forty!" They both laughed. Even though I'd just moved here a few months ago, I'd heard this back-and-forth routine many times. Lily had more relatives living and working in Stellamar than the ocean had shells. They seemed to run everything, except, it turned out, the arcade.

"We could try to win it together," Lily suggested. "The four of us all play and do amazing and then pool our tickets together."

"I'm in." Miranda dropped her token into the slot. Ten wooden baseball-size balls rolled down the chute.

Lily, Avery, and I each claimed a lane and pushed in a token.

"I got it! Fifty points!" Miranda whooped.

"Seriously? Seriously? What is wrong with me?" Lily stamped her foot next to me. She'd already bowled two balls up the ramp. Zero points flashed on her scoreboard. "Ugh. I was so close to that hundred-point hole."

"That's only there to distract you. Just aim up the middle," Miranda called.

I let the weight of the smooth ball rest in my palm. How many other twelve-year-olds have thrown this ball over the years? I thought. Hundreds, probably. I swung my arm back, then followed through, twisting my wrist slightly the way my dad had taught me. The ball glided into the fifty-point slot.

I rolled the next ball in line. Another fifty.

This got Miranda's attention. "You're good," she said, her surprise obvious.

I shrugged as if it were a natural talent. But it wasn't. Dad and I had spent many nights in the arcade when we had first moved here and didn't know anyone. He showed me how to put the right amount of spin on the little wooden ball.

"Go again!" Avery urged. "Maybe we can win the bear."

I rolled the next ball. Not enough spin. Twenty points.

Lily finished her game and turned to watch. Avery edged closer. I tried to concentrate. Think only about the ball. Empty my mind.

"You are so lame!"

"No, you are. Can't even walk."

"Get your foot out of my way."

I glanced toward the door. A group of boys from our school tumbled in, punching each other in the arms. I saw Jack L. and Luke. But there were others behind them. Was he with them?

I wanted to look. To find his warm brown eyes. His crooked smile. But then what? Nothing, I knew. It'd been a week since he'd even said hi to me in class.

So I focused on the skee-ball lane instead. Visualized the ball's path. In one swift motion, I rolled the wooden ball, watching it hop, then drop into the fifty slot.

"The Harvest Queen is lucky," a familiar voice said behind me.

"Not luck. Skill," I replied, not turning. Not looking at him.

He was here. Next to me.

I reached for another ball. Studied the scuffed ramp while inhaling the faint scent of almonds. I loved that smell. Hosten's soap. I knew that because I'd smelled all the soaps at the drugstore last week until I found the right one. Hosten's comes in a three-pack. It was Jayden's soap, I was sure.

Avery giggled. Jack said something to her I couldn't hear.

I tossed the ball. It veered far to the right. Zero points.

"Luck," he said again.

"You messed me up." I turned, pretending to be angry.

"I'm sorry, Your Royal Highness."

I cringed. "Don't call me that," I said. "That's over." Two weeks ago, I was crowned Harvest Queen for the school dance. Most of Stellamar Middle School seemed to have forgotten already, except for a few mean girls in the eighth grade who blamed me for ruining their quest to be even more popular than they already are. And him. He brought it up almost every time he saw me. I think he just thought it was funny.

It was, I guess, if you really know me. The real me.

The title, the wearing the crown at the dance, hey, even going to the dance, was so not me. I only did it to help someone. I never thought I'd win.

But does he know me that well? I wondered. There was still so much about Jayden Mendes I didn't know. Didn't understand.

"I have twenty more tokens. Let's take photos," Lily announced.

"Yes! Let's go!" Avery squealed. She grabbed my hand, tugging me across the arcade to the photo booth. I tripped along, guessing the bear-dog quest had been called off. Miranda followed too.

The four of us piled into the narrow booth. Miranda's long legs dangled outside the curtain, as she and Lily squeezed onto the metal bench. Avery and I perched on their laps, trying not to block their faces. Lily began giggling and couldn't stop. Her laughter was contagious. Avery started snorting.

The photo strip slid from the slot, revealing all of us doubled over with laughter. I looked ridiculous. We shot different combinations. Lily and Avery. Lily and Miranda. Lily and me. Lily had a thing for the photo booth. One wall in her bedroom was covered with hundreds of photo booth strips that she'd woven together. She's in every one, smiling broadly. That pretty much sums up Lily. The center of everything.

"Coming in!" Jack called. He and Luke barreled into the booth. Lily and Avery tried unsuccessfully to push them out.

Garrett and Jayden stood outside the booth. Garrett yanked the pale blue curtain closed. "Time to get cozy!"

Luke flailed his leg out and kicked Garrett in the shin. "Grow up, man!" He opened the curtain and they all tumbled out. Then Miranda and Jack took a photo, pretending to fight. Avery pulled Garrett into the booth next, both making monster faces.

"Our turn," Jayden said suddenly. He nudged me into the booth with his shoulder. I glanced at Lily, who wiggled her eyebrows at me. She knew I liked Jayden.

I slid across the metal bench until my right side pressed against the wall. For a moment, I sat in the little capsule alone. Waiting. Jayden seemed oddly frozen. Then, as if making up his mind about something, he stepped in and sat right beside me. Someone pulled the cotton curtain closed.

I had never been so close to him.

The sleeve of his black T-shirt touched my gray sweatshirt. I gulped. The sound from my throat seemed to echo loudly in our little metal box.

I bit my lip. Should I say something? What?

"Hey," he said softly, turning to look at me.

"Hey." I was too scared to look at him. I studied my Converse. The right shoelace dragged on the corrugated metal floor.

"You need to move over."

"Huh?" If I moved my left hand an inch I would brush his hand. So close.

"Only half your head's in the frame. Look." He raised his hand to the monitor that showed our faces. My blond hair and blue eyes seemed so pale next to his caramel skin and thick brown hair.

I inched closer to him, praying he couldn't feel me tremble. I tried to look natural, to smile. I wanted this photo to look good. The monitor counted down.

Ten . . . nine . . .

The air in our box grew warmer. Heavier. I could smell him. Almond soap. So close.

Eight . . .

But something else too. Something sour.

Seven . . . six . . .

Hot. So hot. The rotten smell clung to my nose and crept along the back my throat. I needed fresh air.

Five . . .

Where was Jayden? My vision blurred. I could no longer sense his body next to me. It was as if someone had wedged a board between us. I struggled to turn my head. The air felt as thick as mud.

Four . . . three . . .

Jayden. He was still here.

But someone sat between us.

Someone I recognized.

Someone who sent a chill down my spine.

I pressed my palms into my jeans, wanting to scream. Knowing I couldn't.

We weren't alone.

Two . . .

Jayden's older brother.

He'd been dead for seven years.

Dead.

But I could see him. Smell him. Feel him.

Dead. But here with us.

I had this weird bond with the dead that none of

my friends knew about. I can't tell them about it. Can't let them know. So I couldn't scream. I had to hold it in.

Lily couldn't know I saw spirits.

Jayden couldn't know Marco was here with us.

One . . .

The camera clicked. The flash illuminated the booth, as the force of Marco's spirit shoved me. With nowhere to go but into the wall, I doubled over. The raised diamond pattern on the floor danced before me.

The curtain yanked open. Lily's smiling face pushed in. "Let me see the—" She stopped when she caught sight of me. "Are you okay?"

I raised my head slowly, still dizzy. Jayden eyed me, confused. The faint outline of his dead brother now stood outside the curtain. Arms crossed. Dark hoodie. Shorts. Glaring eyes. Challenging me.